healed

sugar and
spice ink

BY
EVAN
GRACE

healed

sugar and spice ink

BY EVAN GRACE

dedication

To Jim
for giving me my happily ever after

definition of HEALED

To describe a tattoo two to four weeks after the tattoo has been applied, giving the client's skin time to accept the now settled tattoo.

one

HEIDI

I pin my hair up on top of my head and give it a quick spray. I pull the illuminating powder and contour brush out of my makeup bag. I add some to my forehead and above my cheekbones. I grab Greta's setting spray and quickly use it on my face.

"You look hot, girl," Greta says from behind me. She grabs my lipstick and quickly dabs it on my lips before stepping back. "There, perfection."

Out of the Collins kids, I'm the baby in the family. Greta is a year and a half older than me, but she's my best friend and roommate. I turn back toward the mirror. "Are you sure?"

"Yes, you know I wouldn't tell you, you looked great unless I meant it. I went through your closet and found the perfect outfit." My sister is a fashionista and has a good eye for style.

She disappears out of the bathroom, and I follow her into my bedroom. On my bed are my black low rider wide-leg tuxedo pants and a silver top that hugs my breasts, making them look bigger. Lord knows I could use all the help I can get.

Since I'm the youngest, the boobs were all taken up by the time I came along. I take off my robe and pull on some pink satin panties and a matching bra. I grab my perfume, spray some in front of me, and walk through it.

I get dressed and slip on a pair of black stiletto sling backs. Looking in the mirror, I feel confident and sexy. My plan is to pick up some hot football player and have some much-needed fun.

That's what I need, to have fun. Over the past couple of years, I've spent most of my time building my clientele at the studio and proving to my sisters that I deserved my spot there.

I head into the living room and find Greta standing in front of the mirror, fiddling with her hair. I love my sister, but I can totally admit that I'm jealous of her. She's tall, lean, has gorgeous long, wavy brown hair, and is beautiful inside and out.

Her dress is a mixture of pinks, creams, and browns. It's a long, flowy maxi dress with long sleeves and a slit in the front. She's wearing brown thick-heeled sandals, which compliment her Boho chic style.

She smiles when she sees me. "Damn, I knew that outfit would look great. I ordered our Uber, so we should probably head downstairs."

We grab our purses, lock up, and head downstairs. Tonight is a party for Nick's arena football team. He invited us so we could hang with our sister, Sierra, I'm sure.

When we reach *Blaze*, a man in an all-black suit opens the door for us and holds out his hand, helping each of us out. We step inside and head up a beautiful staircase to the space where the party is at.

We grab some champagne before searching out our family.

"Look at all these hot men," Greta leans down and whispers in my ear.

I cover my mouth as I giggle, but then I sober up. The one and only serious boyfriend I ever had was a football player, a quarterback, and that asshole broke my heart.

Greta moves to stand in front of me. "What's that look for?" She tips her head to the side, looking closely at me.

I give her my best fake smile. "Nothing, just admiring the view." Yes, these men are all hot, but I have no desire to hook up with a football player. "Let's go find everyone." I take a sip of my champagne and thread my arm through hers, and we walk through the crowd, looking for our family.

The party is in full swing, and I glance around the room. There truly are hot guys everywhere. The players we've met have been nice. Several of them have been vying for Greta's attention, but of course they would because she's a babe. I haven't decided if there are any men that I want to speak to yet. Nick calls someone named Colton over, and my stomach pitches, which is stupid because there are a lot of guys out there named Colton.

I turn toward Nick, and that's when my heart stops, and my stomach drops. Colton Winters is standing in front of me for the first time in five years. "Heidi." Just hearing my name on his lips has me turning and running down the stairs.

Outside, I run down the street with Colton calling my name, but all I can hear are the words he spoke to me five years ago. *"Heidi, I just don't love you anymore. This is over."* I stop, panting for breath and holding my side due to a stitch.

Colton stops in front of me, but I don't think—I just react, slapping him across the face. "Stay away from me," I grit out. "I just don't love you anymore." I throw those words back at him and flag down a cab, climbing inside when it pulls up to the curb before he can follow me.

It's not until I'm safely back in my apartment that I finally fall apart. I lock myself in my bedroom and grab a box from the back of my closet. Peeling the lid off, I feel the tears fill my eyes.

The first picture was from our eighth-grade graduation. Colton was behind me with his arms around me—both of us smiling widely at the camera. God, we were just babies, and I still had braces.

No one thought we'd last back then, but we proved them wrong, over and over, with each passing year. I wanted to marry him—I wanted to have his children, and I almost did until that slipped away as well.

In a matter of two months I lost him, and then I lost the baby I was carrying. I never told anyone about the second, and I never will. I honestly don't know what it is about us Collins women, but three of us have found ourselves at one point knocked-up and single. Well, Sierra isn't single; she may say she is, but Nick follows her around like a lovesick fool. I can't wait to see it when she realizes she loves him too.

I focus on the pictures. Shit, I took so many. Our whole relationship is in this box in the form of pictures. My favorite is one that was taken right before Colton broke up with me—the night I'm sure our child was conceived.

"How many people are going with you?" Mom asks as I carry my sleeping bag and backpack downstairs.

I shrug. "I don't know. Maybe three or four. Colton's the one who set this up." Ugh… I hate lying to my mom, but with graduation getting close, we're going to be so busy. Colton and I just want one night alone.

We love camping, so we're going, just the two of us, for a romantic getaway, sleeping under the stars.

Mom gets close, lowering her voice. "I know you're having sex, but promise me you're being careful."

I roll my eyes. "I am. We are; I promise."

My parents found out we were having sex when we were sixteen. One night when they were out, Colton was over, and things were getting very physical between us. Miles had come home to surprise us, and surprise us he did. Poor Colton got chased out of the house, naked, by my overprotective big brother.

He, of course, called our parents, who then came home and chewed us out before calling Colton's mom and dad. There was a lot of yelling, some crying, and then talking.

Colton shows up as I reach the bottom of the stairs. He knocks and then comes right in. "Hey, babe." He leans down to kiss me.

God, he is so hot, but he's so much more than that too. He's kind, loving, funny, and so freaking smart it's scary.

Bam, bam, bam... "Heidi are you okay?" Greta asks from outside my door, pulling me from my trip down memory lane. "Honey, open the door."

"G-go away, Greta. I'm fine. I just want to be left alone." I sit quietly and pray that she goes away.

"Are you sure?" She's quiet for a minute. "Was that the first time you've seen Colton since you broke up?"

Does she mean when *he* broke up with me, shattering my heart into unfixable pieces? I don't answer her because I'm afraid of what might come out of my mouth.

I can hear her sigh from the other side of the door. "I'll leave you alone for now, but I love you, and I'm here for you."

I quickly grab my pillow from my bed, bury my face in it, and sob.

I cringe when I look in the mirror. My eyes are bloodshot, and the bluish-purple hue under my eyes is in stark contrast to my pale skin.

After brushing my teeth, I climb into the shower and let the hot water run over my tired, sore body. I fell asleep the night before on the floor next to the box of pictures. The trip down memory lane stirred up a lot of shit I didn't want to deal with, and now it's plaguing my mind.

My soapy hand slides down my body and stops on my lower abdomen. I wanted our baby so bad, and even though Colton had left, he left me with a part of him that I had planned to love forever. Hell, I still love our baby even though I'd just barely found out I was pregnant when I miscarried.

Climbing out after I rinse off, I wrap a towel around my body. I spray some leave-in conditioner in my hair and then run my comb through it. Back in my room, I get dressed in sweat shorts and a Pearl Jam concert tee.

I blow dry my hair and throw it into a ponytail. I pass by Greta's open door and see she's still asleep. Quickly sticking my feet into a pair of flip flops, I grab my purse and head outside, locking the door behind me.

I drive around for a while, ignoring my ringing cell phone. I'm sure it's one of my sisters, but I'm not ready to talk yet—especially about Colton.

God, he's aged well. Gone was the boy with a softness to his face, and in front of me was the man he is now, all chiseled gorgeousness. His dark blond hair was cut short on the sides and a little longer on top. It still has that wave to it. I'd spend hours running my fingers through his hair.

He reminds me of a blond-haired, brown-eyed Tom Brady. He has that tall, lean body and the dimple in his fucking chin. I whip into the parking lot of the local coffee shop and climb out of my car.

Inside, I order an Earl Gray tea and a chocolate croissant. I grab a seat in front of the fireplace since it's chilly outside, and I forgot a jacket. The barista brings my stuff to me and places it on the table next to the chair.

I thank her and then put a little Splenda and cream in my tea. Taking a sip, I sigh happily as the warm liquid runs down my throat. Staring blindly at the flickering flames, I can't help but wonder where Colton's been these past five years.

Nope, not going to go there. I pick my croissant, moaning as I bite into the sweet, flaky pastry. I won't lie—I eat the entire thing in about three huge bites. After I finish my tea, I head out.

I have no destination in mind, but after a while I pull up in front of our old high school. In the last five years, they've added a performing arts wing and updated the football field. I spent a lot of time on the bleachers watching Colton practice and then watching him play every Friday night. When I ran track, he was always there on the sidelines cheering me on.

The cheerleaders used to hit on him all of the time, but he only had eyes for me. I put my car in drive, leaving those memories behind. A thought occurs to me—does he have a girlfriend? Is he married, a Dad?

My eyes burn, and it feels like someone is sitting on my chest. "Nope, I don't care about any of that," I whisper to myself because now I'm crazy.

I realize that I'm by the studio, so I pull into the parking lot and park. I pull my keys out and head inside. After turning the alarm off, I lock the front door.

My flip flops slap against the tile floor as I head back to the office. I stop in front of the mirror and pull down my t-shirt until the tattoo my sisters all tried to talk me out of comes into view. I got it about six months after he left. *"Love doesn't live here anymore."* It's in a swirly design right over my heart.

I needed that daily reminder to not fall in love. I've dated some in the past five years. I've even had sex, but it's always been mediocre. Colton and I had years and years to learn about each other and what the other liked. We may have been teenagers, but the sex was always mind-blowing.

"Ugh... stop thinking about him, idiot." Great, now I'm talking to myself. I flop down on the loveseat and pull my phone out of my purse. I have several missed calls and texts.

| **Greta:** | Where are you? Are you okay? |
| **Greta:** | If you don't answer me, I'm calling in the cavalry. |

Fuck, she did it too.

Mona:	Sweetie, please check in. Are you okay? Greta told us last night that you were home and locked in your room. He came back to the party and looked really sad.
Sierra:	Where are you? Please check in.
Miles:	Do I need to kick his ass? I'll do it.

I smile because I do love my family even though they drive me nuts. You'd think it would be hard working together, day in and day out, but thankfully we're close. Although sometimes Mona will try to mother me—you know, with her being the oldest she has always taken it upon herself to watch out for me.

I type out a quick group text.

Heidi:	Guys, I'm okay; I promise. I just need some alone time to think. I love you all.
Mona:	Love you too, sweetheart
Sierra:	What she said ;) Love you, babe.
Miles:	I'll still kick his ass if you want.

Greta: Love you.

I tuck my phone into my bag and lay on my back with my legs hanging over the arm of the loveseat.

two

COLTON

I do a back squat with my fellow teammate Tyrell spotting me. It's been two weeks since I saw Heidi and my heart started beating again. I know that sounds corny, but it's true.

Leaving Heidi five years ago was one of the hardest things I've ever done, but I had a good reason. I thought I was protecting her from an uncertain future. Fuck, but she's even more beautiful than when we were younger.

The look on her face after she slapped me will haunt me forever. Her repeating the words that I had said to her back then hurt worse than any hit I've ever taken in football.

"Fuck, Colt. You're a fucking beast." Tyrell squats behind me with his hands hovering under the barbell. I stand up and step forward, placing the barbell in the rack.

My workouts have definitely gotten better in the past two weeks because I've had copious amounts of stress to work off. I slap Tyrell on the back as we switch spots, and I spot him; of course he has to add about a hundred more pounds to the barbell.

Once he finishes his set, we grab a couple bottles of water and chug them down. "You have plans tonight?" he asks.

Coming to this team right before the start of the season was a risky move, but Ty has been the one to make the transition super easy for me. He and his wife, Monique, have had me over a lot. My parents are still in New York for the time being, so it's been nice having home-cooked meals. Ty and I have shared many a beer on his back porch—enough for me to tell him all about Heidi and why I left her.

"Nah, I was just going to pick up a steak or something."

Tyrell follows me into the locker room. "Come over for dinner. Moni will be happy to feed you."

His wife is amazing, and in her opinion a home-cooked meal solves many a problem. Don't get me wrong, I enjoy spending time with them. In such a short period of time, Ty has become a good friend, but I hate feeling like I'm encroaching on their family time.

"Sure, thanks. I'll bring her favorite wine and cupcakes for the kids."

He slaps me on the back, and then we head to the showers—separately of course.

I scroll through Heidi's Instagram page. She's always had a thing for pink, and I'm not surprised that her hair has been various shades of it over the past couple of years.

I look through her pictures, and I don't see a boyfriend or a husband. I won't lie—it makes me happy knowing she is single. It gives me the slightest twinge of hope—hope that I could win her back.

When I tell her the reason I left, she'll understand... I hope. It killed me to make her feel like I didn't love her anymore, but it was the only way to sever ties completely.

I stop on a picture of Heidi in a bikini. She's always had a beautiful body, but now—now it's even better. Her athletic build is curvier and her breasts are fuller. Heidi has the body of a woman.

I exit out of the app because I'm nothing but a creepy stalker. In my bedroom, I grab the frame that's on my nightstand. It's a picture of Heidi and me the summer before our senior year in high school.

Heidi was in a pink sundress, her blonde hair was up in a high ponytail, and her feet were bare. I was sitting behind her, my arms pulling her back against my chest. We were babies, but I knew I wanted to spend the rest of my life with her.

Unfortunately, fate had other plans, and honestly, I didn't expect to live past the age nineteen. It made it easier to leave her, knowing I was leaving her to live the life she deserved.

I put the picture back on the nightstand. After I shut off the lamp, I crawl underneath my covers and watch the shadows dance across the ceiling. I'm not sure how to approach Heidi, but I need to tread lightly; otherwise, she'll never let me back in.

With everything on my mind, it's a long time before I fall asleep.

I pull into the parking lot of Sugar and Spice, Ink and park my SUV. I'm not sure what I'm doing here, but I wanted to see her. In the past month I've only seen Heidi a couple of times, and each time I've tried to talk to her she runs in the other direction as fast as she can.

Inside, the place is buzzing with activity. There are people in the waiting area. Greta sits behind the counter with a platinum blonde. I spot Mona and Sierra both working on people, but I don't see Heidi.

Greta looks up and crosses her arms over her chest. "What are you doing here? Heidi doesn't want to see you."

"I just want a chance to talk to her. I swear I'm not trying to hurt her, but there are some things that I need to say to her... please." I hope she can see that I'm sincere. "Please, Greta."

She sighs. "She's in the office down the hall, but if she tells you to leave, leave."

"Thank you." Every step I take down the hall my stomach starts to turn violently, but I breathe through it. I reach the open door and find Heidi sitting behind the desk; her cotton candy pink hair is twisted up into an intricate knot on top of her head.

She's leaned over the desk, drawing, and she's so focused on what she's doing, she's oblivious to me watching her. When Heidi used to be focused on something, her tongue would poke out from the corner of her lips, which it's doing right now.

I could watch her forever, but I know I can't, so I knock on the door frame to get her attention. She looks up, and her eyes widen in obvious surprise and then apparent disgust.

"What are you doing here?" She slowly stands. "You need to leave, Colton."

I shake my head. "I can't. I can't leave until you agree to meet me so we can talk. I know I don't have the right to ask anything of you, but if you give me the chance to explain, then maybe you'll understand." I walk further into the office and come around the desk to stand in front of her.

"What makes you think you deserve that chance?" Heidi backs away from me, or tries because I match her step for step, advancing on her until we're almost chest to chest.

"I know I don't deserve a chance, but I want it—I need it. Please, Heidi. I promise that after you hear me out, if you still want me gone, I'll be gone." I sound so fucking desperate right now, but I don't care.

She doesn't speak right away, but so many emotions cross her face while I wait for her to answer. I want to pull her into my arms and hold her tight as I tell her that I never stopped loving her. Every minute I was away from her felt like an eternity.

My parents didn't understand my decision to end things with Heidi and tried multiple times to talk me out of it. I just didn't want to saddle her with everything that was about to happen.

She lets out a resigned sigh. "Fine, we can talk. After that, I don't want to see you again." Heidi scoots past me and then practically runs out of the office.

I'm not feeling super hopeful, but she did agree to meet with me. I'll tell her everything, and just maybe she'll give me a second chance.

three

HEIDI

I clean up my station after my last client left. It was a cover-up job. She got her husband's name tattooed on her wrist, and he thanked her by fucking their nanny. She kicked his ass out, and I covered his name with the flower, Edelweiss, which means courage.

She thought it was fitting because she had the courage to leave her marriage that was unhealthy.

My mind wanders to Colton. I've agreed to hear him out. This coming Sunday, which is five days from now, he and I will be face-to-face for the last time. Maybe then I'll finally be able to move on; that's all I want.

I jump when Greta hops onto the client chair. "Shit, sorry. I didn't mean to scare you." We're the last ones here tonight, which sucks, but Greta and I said we'd stay. Mona has Iris and Max at home, and Sierra's preggers.

I shake my head. "That's okay. My mind was wondering. Do we have anyone else coming in tonight?"

"Nope, I think we're safe to shut it down." Greta hops off the chair and checks that everything is shut off. I grab the deposit to drop off at the bank on the way back to our apartment.

Once we have our bags, we head out to my blue Jeep Wrangler. This was our brother Miles' first car, and he took really good care of it. When I got it, it slowly became banged up. I'll be the first to admit I'm a terrible driver, and since I've owned the jeep it's gotten covered in lots of scratches and dings.

"What happens when you see Colton this weekend?" Greta asks out of the blue. Until now she's given me my space when it's come to him.

"Nothing happens. I listen to what he has to say, and then we're over... for good." I won't admit to her that the thought makes me sad. I love him, always have and always will. I know that makes me seem pathetic, but I don't care—I feel what I feel.

Greta drops it, and we make our way home.

My tennis shoes slap against the pavement as I run along the bike path. Lady Gaga blasts through my earbuds; it's the perfect distraction from my thoughts.

As I push myself harder and harder, I drive out thoughts of Colton, our baby, and what could've been. I also can't help but think about our upcoming talk. Why did he disappear? Did I cross his mind, at all? No... I don't care about that.

By the time I make it back to my apartment, my legs feel like jelly, and I have a stitch in my side. Before I go up, I do some stretches and then wait for the nausea to pass.

After a quick shower, I make myself a sandwich and can only choke about half of it down. I'm closing the studio tonight, and I don't have to be in until three. I decide to do something I rarely do and take a nap.

I end up only sleeping for thirty minutes, but apparently that was all I needed. I crawl out of bed and get ready for my shift. I brush out my hair and throw it into a high ponytail. I pull on my favorite Sugar and Spice, Ink black t-shirt, red leggings, and my newer pair of black Nikes.

I make myself an iced coffee, pour it into my travel mug, grab my bag, and head to work. The studio parking lot is full when I arrive, which makes me smile.

I smile at Lainey as I enter the lobby. She is our apprentice, who is manning the front desk today. She's been an amazing addition, and she's already begun tattooing her own clients. Of course, for now it's only small pieces, but she's damn good.

I take my stuff back to the office and then get ready for my first client.

By the end of the day my back is sore. I worked on the outline of a huge back piece, which means I was bent over for a long time. Once I lock up, I head home. I step inside and lock the door. In the kitchen I grab the bottle of Moscato and pour myself a healthy amount in a wine glass.

In my bedroom I place the wine on my nightstand and change into my sleep shirt, which is Colton's old

Jamison High football team t-shirt. I only kept it because it's so soft to sleep in. Of course, most of the print has come off the shirt, but I still love it.

I get settled into my bed, leaning against a stack of pillows and grabbing my e-reader. I'm reading a college romance about a single mom and a jock who meet and fall in love. By the time I finish my glass of wine, I'm reading the epilogue and smiling widely.

Even though I had my heart broken, I do believe in love. Mona found it with Joaquin, and once Sierra admits she loves Nick, they'll probably live happily ever after.

Speaking of my sister Sierra... We had an incident not long after I saw Colton for the first time.

Sierra walks into the office. "What are you doing?"

I look up at her and smile, and I try to hide the sadness I feel. "I'm uploading pictures onto all of our social media accounts." I look her over. "How are you feeling? I've noticed you haven't been as sick."

"I'm feeling better. We found lots of tricks to keep me from getting nauseous." She sits across from me. "What's up with Colton?"

My body stiffens, and I keep my eyes on the laptop. "Nothing's up."

"That didn't seem like nothing."

"We dated. We broke up—the end." I continue to type on the keyboard.

She leans forward. "Honey, we all thought you guys were going to be together forever."

I look up at her, irritation quickly coursing through me. "So did I." She opens her mouth to respond, but I stop her. "I don't need or want the advice of someone who got knocked-up by her fuck buddy." Her body jerks like it's been hit.

I grab my bag and storm out of the office. I climb into my Jeep, and as I pull out of the parking lot, I look in my rearview mirror and see Sierra running out of the studio.

My phone pings when I'm a block away, and I know right away it's my sister.

> **Sierra:**   I'm sorry. I shouldn't have pried. You both just looked so sad. I love you, Heidi Ho.

Poor Sierra was just concerned about me, but she didn't deserve to be treated that way by me.

Luckily, she forgave me, and all was forgotten, but that is the way it has always been for us Collins girls. We fight, fight, fight, but always make up quickly.

After shutting my e-reader off, I carry my empty wineglass into the kitchen and then head into the bathroom to brush my teeth and wash my face. I step back into my room while I'm rubbing my moisturizer into my face.

As soon as I'm lying down my mind does what it usually has a tendency to do now that he's back, and I begin to think about Colton—especially the night he ended things.

Something's going on with Colton. For the past week he's been quiet, standoffish, and easily angered. I mean, he's never hurt me, but he's constantly on edge. Butterflies take flight in my belly as I wait on the porch for him to pick me up to talk.

It feels like he's getting ready to break up with me. What I don't know is why. We've been making plans for our future—a future he swore he wanted with me. When his truck pulls up, he doesn't get out like he usually does.

I make my way toward him and feel like my feet are filled with lead. I take a deep breath and climb in. "Hey," I say quietly,

He doesn't respond; instead, he throws his truck into drive, and we take off. We drive around in uncomfortable silence. Colton finally pulls into the parking lot of Woodland Park, which is near our high school.

I wait and wait for whatever is about to happen. The desire to throw up hits me hard, but I ignore it and steady my breathing. I can't take the impending doom anymore and whisper harshly. "Just say it already."

"I want to break up with you." His voice is flat, no emotion at all. "This is over."

Deep down I knew this was coming, but hearing those words come out of his mouth hurt. "Why?" My eyes burn, but I won't cry, or at least not in front of him. "Answer me, Colton. I deserve to know."

Colton turns to look at me. "I just don't love you anymore."

My heart breaks into a million pieces. How could he say that after everything we've been through? I've loved him so long; how could he destroy us so callously?

I hop out of his truck, ignoring him calling my name and take off running. I make it home and slam through the back door, ignoring my family and flying up the stairs to my room. Once I'm safely inside, I finally let the tears fall.

"Heidi? Heidi, wake up?"

I open my eyes to see Greta sitting next to me. I must've fallen asleep. I push myself up. "What's up?" I ask.

"You were crying in your sleep." Concern is etched on my sister's beautiful face.

That's when I realize my cheeks are wet. "Sorry. I'm okay. I promise." I give her what I hope is a reassuring smile.

"Okay, goodnight." She leans in and kisses my cheek.

I lie back down, afraid to fall back asleep, but too tired to fight it.

four

COLTON

I throw the football to Marcus, our wide receiver, and watch him run it in for a touchdown, winning the game for us. We all run down the field toward him, my heart pounding in my chest.

After we all exchange backslapping hugs, we run toward the tunnel to head to the locker rooms. Coach Stan comes in and signals for all of us to be quiet. I sit in front of my locker, ready to get this uniform off.

"I won't keep you guys long, but I just wanted to tell you that I'm so fucking proud of you. Colton, I've never seen you play better or harder. You've been an asset to the team. Let's meet Monday to go over game tape. Go celebrate and enjoy a couple days off; you've deserved it."

I head to the showers, stripping out of my sweat-saturated clothes. The hot water feels great on my muscles, but there's a line of players waiting for the showers, so I quickly wash and then step out. We're going out tonight to celebrate our win.

Once I'm dressed in my suit, Tyrell comes walking over. "Great fucking game, Colt. Your arm is a cannon."

We share a backslapping hug. "Thanks, man. Look at you; you didn't let anyone get past you."

He rode with me, so we make our way out to my truck. We're all meeting for dinner at Nick's restaurant, *Nicholas*. Having a restauranteur as a co-owner of the team definitely has its benefits.

When we get there, we head into the private room. I'm thankful to be out and not thinking about tomorrow. I'm not ashamed to admit that I'm scared. Heidi and I belong together, and I'm worried that I damaged things irreparably, and she'll never take me back.

We exchange handshakes and backslapping hugs with the other guys. As we sit, our waiter takes our drink and dinner order, before he disappears.

He returns with our drinks and the waitress helping him flirts with every single one of us, but most of us friendly, and not overly so. It takes a bit, but then our food is brought out, and I waste no time digging into my steak. While we eat, some of the guys decide to go out for drinks after dinner. Usually I pass, but I could definitely use the distraction.

Instead of going to a club, we settle on a little hole in the wall bar. No one knows us there, and we're able to drink beer and play pool. Ty and I don't stay too late, and after I drop him off at his home, I head home. It's a long time before sleep finds me.

While staring at the shadows dancing across my ceiling, I go through every scenario that could go down tomorrow.

"What time is Heidi coming over?" Mom asks. I called her to get her advice if I should make Heidi dinner when she comes over.

I look at the clock. "She should be here in a half hour." I'm so worried she won't show up. Earlier I texted her my address, and the only reason I know she got it is because it said read. Other than that, she didn't respond.

"Oh, honey, I hope it goes well. If she lets you, give her a hug for me." Mom has been rooting for me since I moved back here. Dad has too, but Mom and Heidi were really close. "Call me and let me know."

"I will. Love you, Mom." She says the same before we disconnect. I decide to make some guacamole, her favorite, and pull down the chips. I wanted to get her some alcohol, but I realized it wouldn't be a good idea, especially if our conversation goes badly.

I want to keep things casual so I'm wearing dark gray track pants, a blue thermal shirt, and bare feet. I run my fingers through my hair, a nervous habit I have. I pace while I wait for her to show up.

"She's not coming," I whisper to myself. Heidi should've been here ten minutes ago. I want to text her, but I don't want to appear eager or demanding. Deep down I knew this was a possibility. She owes me nothing.

I sit on the edge of the couch, rest my elbows on my knees, and cover my face with my hands. I've lost her for good. I don't know why I even thought that I could win her back.

I need to move on—I need to let her go.

Knock, knock, knock. My head flies up, and my heart starts to race. I stand and quickly wipe my sweaty palms on my thighs. I reach the door and take a deep breath, before pulling the door open.

Heidi takes my breath away. She's dressed in an off-the-shoulder hot pink sweater, black leggings, and hot pink Vans hi-tops. Her cotton candy pink hair is up in a crazy looking knot on top of her head.

I move back, letting her step inside before shutting the door behind her. "I didn't think you were coming."

She turns around to face me. "I got here early and parked down the street, debating if I should go through with this or not. I finally decided I better get this over with."

Heidi looks around my sparsely decorated living room. I know she sees the pictures of us on the wall, from brace faced pre-teens to two eighteen-year-olds.

"You were always so photogenic," I say from behind her. "I'm glad you came."

She whips around to face me. "The quicker you tell me whatever it is you have to say, the quicker I can be gone."

Ouch... I wince, but I deserve it. When I ended our relationship, I thought I was doing the right thing. No matter how much it hurt, I knew I had to sever ties with her completely.

"Please come sit with me." I grab her hand, and thankfully she doesn't try to pull it from mine. Once we're sitting on the sofa, I turn so I'm facing her full on. I grab both of her hands. "There is no easy way to say this." I take a deep breath. "Remember when I started getting tired all the time? I had those weird bruises and was just sick for like two weeks."

I let go of one of her hands to rub it over my hair. "Heidi, it was cancer."

five

HEIDI

"Heidi, it was cancer."

"What? Cancer?" I pull my hands from his before standing. "Why didn't you tell me?"

Colton stands and moves until he's right in front of me. My heart pounds in my chest. I look him over closely and begin to remember how sick he'd gotten. We noticed the bruises that would pop up overnight—dark purple bruises that looked painful.

"Ahem… wh-what kind of cancer did you have?" I step back from him, because he keeps getting closer to me.

He grabs my hand. "Acute lymphoblastic leukemia."

"Acute Lymphoblastic Leukemia? I don't understand why you didn't tell me." I walk around him and sit down. He follows suit and, again, grabs my hand.

"I was in shock. I don't think it sank in at first. Mom and Dad both started crying, and all I thought was that I was going to die and leave you. Mom's family, if you remember, are from New York, and they decided to find a hospital there that specialized in cancer treatment."

I blink rapidly to stop the tears that threaten to spill over. "W-why didn't you ask me to go with you?" As much as sadness wants to wash through me, I don't let it; instead, I let the anger move through me. "Y-you told me you didn't love me anymore." I jump up from the couch, pacing back and forth in front of him. "I would've taken care of you."

Colton stands and moves in front of me to stop my pacing. "I didn't want that for you," he whispers.

My hand flies up, slapping him across the face. I then jump on him until I'm wrapped around him like a spider monkey. Then my lips are on his. I spear his hair with my fingers, gripping the strands in my fists.

He immediately takes over the kiss, his tongue brushing mine. I feel it as we move through his home. When my back hits his mattress, we begin to rip each other's clothes off.

Suddenly he's thrusting inside of me, both of us moaning into the others mouth. It's urgent, painful, and amazing all at once. I begin to cry, and he stops moving. "No... keep going," I whisper brokenly against his lips.

Colton moves again, but not with the same urgency as before. I push on his shoulders until we roll, and I'm on top. I ride him hard, loving the way he feels inside of me. The lovers I've had since him have been mediocre at best, but I think that had to do more with the love Colton and I felt for each other.

I cry out as he pushes himself up, grabbing my waist, and sucking a nipple into his mouth. I hug him to my chest as he continues his oral assault. In no time I'm coming, moaning and babbling incoherently as I ride the blissful wave.

He flips us over, slides his arms under my thighs, and spreads me wide as he pounds into me at a punishing pace. He pumps once, then twice before burying himself to the hilt. I feel it as he bathes my channel with his cum.

Colton stays buried deep inside me as we both fight to catch our breath. He brushes my hair that's fallen from the knot on top of my head back from my face. It's a tender touch, one that I've longed for since the last time I saw him.

After he pulls his softening cock out of me, he kisses me on the lips. "I'll be right back." I watch him climb off the bed. Fuck me, his body is impressive, but then it always has been. He's tall, lean, and even better than when he was a teenager.

The moment he leaves the bedroom, I jump off his bed, getting dressed faster than I ever have before. I bolt for the living room, grabbing my shoes and don't even bother to put them on. I'm in my car speeding away from his house.

"What did I do?" I whisper to myself over and over.

I ignore my ringing phone, knowing exactly who it is. I stop at the grocery store and, after putting my shoes back on, go right to the liquor aisle, grabbing a bottle of Rose. I'm going to really need this tonight.

Inside my apartment, I find my sister lying on the couch reading our brother's latest crime novel. She lays the book down and takes one look at me and the bottle of wine in my hand. "Oh shit."

I then start to cry.

It's been two days since I had sex with Colton. I know I'm a chicken, hiding from him, but sleeping with him brought back too many emotions I've kept buried deep.

I know we need to finish our talk, or do we? It's clear I'm not over him, but where do we go from here? I grab my phone and scroll through the text messages he left after I took off.

Colton: Where did you go?

Ten minutes later he sent another.

Colton: Heidi, please call me. I just
                want to make sure you're okay.

In between the two texts he called me twice. He didn't leave messages, but that's good because if I would've heard his voice, I most certainly would have gone back over there.

Colton: Dammit, please text me back,
                call me, or something.

A half hour later came the last one that night.

Colton: I love you, Heidi. I'm sorry that
                I hurt you, but I swear I
                thought I was doing the right
                thing. We... uh... didn't use any
                protection the other night. I'm
                clean, I swear.

I knew the moment I stood up the other night that we didn't use anything. His cum was running down the inside of my thigh. I've missed the window to take the pill to prevent pregnancy, and I'm not sure if it was accidental or on purpose, but it was definitely stupid not to take it, or for us to use a condom.

I toss my phone on the desk and finish loading our latest finished pieces onto our website and social media platforms. I'm always so impressed when I upload the pictures—we're damn talented.

I get up from the desk and tuck my phone into my back pocket. Out front, Lainey is sitting at the desk. "Hey, girl. Are you all done for the night?" This girl lives and breathes our studio.

Taking her on was one of the best decisions we ever made. She may not be blood, but she's family.

"Yep, but I had nothing else going on, so I decided to stick around and help Greta." She looks at the computer and then up at me. "She has someone coming in to get pierced right before we close."

The door chime sounds, and I turn around to find Colton stepping inside. "What are you doing here?" I walk toward him.

"You wouldn't answer my texts or calls. Are you okay?"

"Let's go into the office." He follows me down the hall and I close the office door behind him. "As you can see, I'm fine."

"Please don't act like you weren't affected by what happened the other night; it insults us both. You felt it too, so don't pretend you didn't."

Ugh, this man if infuriating. "Fine. Yes, I felt it too. Are you happy? The moment our lips met, every feeling, every emotion came rushing back." Colton tries to come toward me, but I hold my hands up. Thankfully he stops. "I would've taken care of you. I would've made sure you knew I was fighting right alongside you."

Tears slide down my cheeks, and I turn away; I don't want him to see me cry.

I feel him as he comes up behind me and then his arms wrap around me, holding me tight. I cry harder as he leans down, pressing his forehead into my neck.

"Shhh, baby. No tears, please. You know I don't like to see you cry," he says as he turns me in his arms so he can hug me closer.

Once I finally get myself under control, I step away from him. "Do you see what being around you is doing to me?" I know it's mean, and I shouldn't have said something like that—especially now that he's looking at me with a hurt look on his face.

Colton doesn't say anything. He nods once and then turns, walks out, shutting the door behind him.

Six

COLTON

I step inside my old high school and am hit with a massive dose of nostalgia. All four years here were the best of my life. Of course, that was because I had my girl. Fuck, just thinking about what she said to me last week... *"Do you see what being around you is doing to me?"*

It was the kill shot, the one that showed me that we were really and truly over. I'd hoped we could start over, but there is so much history there—painful history that is all my fault, and she'll never forgive me.

"Colton Winters." I am pulled from my thoughts and turn to the principal, Mr. Kosher. "It's good to see you, son."

"You too, Mr. Kosher. The school looks exactly the same, but different." I take his outstretched hand, giving it a firm shake.

"Yeah, we've done a little updating. The football field got a major makeover." We stop in front of a display case, and I spot a picture of me with Heidi on my back after we won the state championship our senior year.

"Did the box of Atlanta Fire t-shirts and tickets arrive?" I ask as we walk down the hall.

"Yes, thank you, so much for that. The kids are all excited to come see you play."

I follow him into the main office. There's a woman standing by the counter, and when she turns our way, I can see that she's pretty, with her long brown curls and big green eyes.

"Hi there," she says with a smile before coming toward us with her hand outstretched. "You must be the football player."

Mr. Kosher slaps me on the shoulder. "This is Jamison high's all-star quarterback, Colton Winters. This is one of our teachers."

I shake her offered hand.

Her smile is big and bright. "Pleasure to meet you, I'm Leesa Jones. I teach AP English, and I'm in charge of the fundraiser." Mr. Kosher leaves us, heading back to his office. "If you want to come with me, we can go talk in the teacher's lounge."

I pull the door open for her, and she grins at me as she passes by. I follow her out, and we walk side by side to the lounge. "I always wanted to see what it looked like in here," I say with a laugh.

"Well, today's your lucky day." She opens the door, and I step inside. The space looks like your average breakroom. "Would you like some coffee?"

"Sure, thanks." I take a seat at the table and stare blindly out the window, my mind trying to go to a place I've tried to avoid. I'm so lost in my thoughts that I jerk in surprise when Leesa sets a coffee cup in front of me.

"Sorry. I didn't mean to scare you," she says as she sits across from me.

I shake my head. "Sorry. I spaced out for a minute."

"Girl trouble?" She picks up her cup and takes a drink. "Of course, that's none of my business and probably unprofessional, but my boyfriend tells me I like to meddle in other people's business."

I chuckle. "This place brings back a lot of memories for me. Let's save my girl troubles for another day."

Leesa smiles and nods, then we get to work on the fundraiser.

The water boy hands me a bottle of water as I run off the field, and I squirt a healthy dose into my mouth. We're playing Chicago in the last regular season game before the playoffs begin. and we're up by six with two minutes left on the clock. I just threw a pass that led to a touchdown to put us ahead.

I pace the sideline as I watch our defense stop every pass and run. When there is a little over a minute left on the clock, I run out onto the field. We get into a position, and I shout, "686 Pump F-Stop on two." I throw it to Sean, who catches it, and I watch as he runs it in for a touchdown.

The stadium goes wild, and we all run down the field. We pull our helmets off, thrusting them up in the air. After we celebrate on the field, I do a quick interview with the reporters.

The owners, Gordo and Nick, come down to congratulate us. It's a damn shame that Nick is stepping down, but I heard what happened with one of the cheerleaders, and it almost ruined his relationship with Heidi's sister, the mother of his unborn baby.

We finally head to the locker room, and I strip out of my gear, grab my shower shoes, and head back to get cleaned up. The guys are all rowdy around me, pumped up after our amazing win.

At my locker, I get dressed in my suit and am slipping on my shoes when a few of our defensive lineman stop to talk. "You gonna come out with us tonight?" Draven asks.

Normally I go out with Tyrell and then call it an early night. The single guys usually go out looking to get laid hell; some of the ones in relationships or married look to hook up too. That's not my style. I prefer it mean something.

Which makes me think of Heidi, we were each other's firsts, and I'd hoped we would be each other's last. Fuck, I promised myself I wouldn't go there. "You know what, yeah, I could use a drink." They all look at me with wide eyes. "I know, I know."

I grab my bag and follow them outside. We head to Urban Fusion, which is owned by Nick. They usually put out a spread for the players, food and drinks, and then we usually get our own bartender.

I carry my bottle of Coors Light over to the table I'm sitting at with a couple of players when a blonde comes bouncing over. "Are you guys athletes?"

"We play for the Fire, sweetheart," Bradford, he's part of the offensive line, says. He gives her the smile that gets him girls all the time. "Why don't you join us?"

I shake my head and drink my beer.

"I'm here with my friends," she says as she gives Bradford goo-goo eyes.

"Well, bring them over, but you're all mine." He winks, she giggles and then flounces away.

I stay and have one more drink, even posing for a picture with one of the blonde's friends. I'm beat, so it's time to head home.

I drink down the rest of my beer and say goodbye to my boys. The guys all boo me as I walk away, so I lift my hand and give them the finger. Their laughter follows me out the door.

The sound of my phone pinging over and over pulls me from my sleep. I see that a girl tagged me on Instagram, and people have been commenting on it. I grab my phone and open the app.

I pull the picture up, and it's the one I took with the girl at Urban Fusion last night. If it were up to me, I wouldn't be on social media at all, but it's good for the team and my image.

After I exit out of the app, I see that it's only seven-thirty. I'm awake, so I decide to crawl out of bed. Since I showered last night, I throw some sweats on and then head out to the kitchen to start coffee and make myself a protein shake.

While I chug it down, I turn on the TV. When I'm finished, I toss my shaker bottle into the sink. I pour myself a cup of coffee and head into the living room to watch "Forged in Fire" on Netflix.

The only plans I have for the day is dinner with my parents tonight; other than that I don't plan on moving from this spot. It'll be a nice lazy day—just what I like to do the day after a game.

My phone pings a while later, pulling my attention away from the TV. I pick it up and see it's a text from Leesa.

Leesa:	Hey, Colton, I have some ideas for the fundraiser and was wondering if you wanted to grab lunch.

She has a boyfriend, but hopefully this isn't some ploy to try to make a play for me. She's beautiful, but I'm just not interested.

Colton:	Sure, let me know where. Oh, btw, I have several other players interested in helping.
Leesa:	Great to both. Blake is excited to meet you.

We make plans on where to meet, and then I press play on my show.

seven

HEIDI

I place my hands on Sierra's belly, smiling up at her when the baby kicks her mom's belly. I'm so happy for her and Nick, but then I'm hit with a wave of sadness, thinking about what could've been.

She reaches out and strokes my cheek. "Are you okay, sweetheart? You seem sad."

I'm the youngest out of five. Sierra and Mona were always mother hens to me and Greta. Miles was always the protector of all of us girls. It makes me feel so shitty that I was crappy toward her about Colton.

"Heidi?"

I look up at her, open my mouth, and tell her *everything*. From Colton and my breakup, to the miscarriage, up to sleeping with him last week, and finally the mean shit I said in the office.

I'm crying hard, but it feels good to let it all out. Nick comes home while I'm having my moment. He kisses my sister on the lips and bends down, kissing the top of my head.

Thanks to my two big sisters, I have two more big brothers to love. He disappears further into their apartment, leaving us alone.

I take a deep breath and pull back, wiping the tears from my eyes. "Sorry about that."

Sierra's eyes go soft. "Don't apologize. Why didn't you tell anyone that you were pregnant?"

I shrug. "I'd barely found out myself before I lost it. I didn't think it mattered anymore."

"Honey, you may not have been far along, but that was still your baby. Does Colton know?" I shake my head. "I can't believe he had cancer," she whispers.

"I love him, but I hurt him." I look down at my hands. "The look on his face tells me that it's over. I'm never going to see him again."

"Don't say that. You don't know how he truly fee—" I hold up my hand to stop her from talking.

"You didn't see him; it felt so final when he left."

Sierra grabs my hands and pulls me into a hug. "It doesn't have to be final if you don't want it to be. He thought he was doing the right thing. Take some time and decide if you can live without him. If you can't, then there's your answer."

I kiss her and hug her one more time before patting her belly and then standing. Nick comes out and gives me a hug, then walks me to the door. "You okay?"

I smile up at the built, blond hottie who is so head over heels in love with my sister. "Not yet, but I will be. Take care of your girls."

Nick's face lights up, and it makes me love him for Sierra even more. "Until the day I die." I push up on my tiptoes and kiss his cheek one more time before getting on the elevator, waving to him as the doors slide shut.

Once I'm out of the building, I walk to my car. My stomach growls loudly, reminding me that I haven't eaten today.

I decide to stop at my favorite little coffee shop that has the best chicken and avocado panini. When I pull into the parking lot, I check my bag to see if I have my iPad. I do, so I get out and head inside.

The scent of coffee beans hits me as soon as I walk inside. I stop at the counter and order my sandwich and a matcha iced latte. I grab a chair at the counter and wait for my sandwich.

I sip my drink as I scroll through Instagram and grin when I pull up Greta's story. She's doing one of her makeup tutorials. I love my sissy with all my heart, and thankfully her inner beauty is as strong as her outer beauty.

Her fan base is huge and keeps growing. Of course, with the fans comes the trolls, but she has a thick skin and doesn't let their comments bother her. Usually they're about her tattoos and piercings, how she shouldn't have so many. She brushes it off.

The door dings, and I look around the plant, freezing when I see who is walking in. Colton leads a beautiful brunette inside, and I duck down so they can't see me. Luckily there's a big plant by me, and I'm able to hide.

They stand at the counter talking quietly, and my heart hurts watching him smile at her. Are they on a date? They'd make a beautiful couple—fuck, the words taste like acid on my tongue.

After they order I don't see where they go; all I know is I can't stay here. I can't watch him date, but isn't that what I wanted? I hurt him and pushed him away.

When the girl brings my sandwich I lean in and whisper, "Can I have it to go please?"

She smiles and nods before I watch her wrap it up and then place it in a brown paper bag. I thank her and grab it, and as quick as I can, I practically running until I reach my car.

It's not until I'm almost home that I realize I have tears running down my cheeks. Shit.

My tattoo machine lightly vibrates in my hand as I work on the color of a sleeve. The client is wearing earbuds, listening to an audiobook, and I'm wearing mine, listening to the audiobook of my brother's new release.

Normally I only read romance novels, but I can't *not* read or listen to my brother's books. Plus, it blocks out my thoughts. I haven't been able to stop thinking about Colton or the date he was on. I've constantly punished myself by wondering what they were doing, how their date went, or if he was really into her.

Why does the thought of him getting his happily ever after with someone else hurt so bad? Oh, yeah, because I love him and always will. I let Miles' word flow through me as I finish the color on the cheetah on my client's forearm.

I wipe down the tattoo. I'm still not done, but after two hours I pull my earbuds out and tell her I'm going to take a quick break if she wants to take one too. It will give both of us a chance to get up and stretch.

Lainey grabs her a drink, and I head to the office, stretching my back. I find my sister Mona and her gorgeous man, Joaquin, making out like a couple of teenagers.

"Ewww… I don't want to see this," I squeal and then cover my eyes.

Their laughter makes me smile. "Okay, we're done, *mi cuñada.*" I move my hands from my face and see Joaquin is walking toward me, and I immediately walk into his arms for a hug. "How are you?"

I shrug. "Ahhh… I've been okay, I guess." Before they can comment on that, I ask about the kids. "You know not to show up without those monsters I love." Max and Iris say they're twins now because they're the same age, but obviously biologically they do not share blood. Iris' sperm donor is not involved, and Max's mom takes him whenever the mood strikes, which isn't often.

Oh, well. I say it's their loss because they don't get to know these incredible kids.

"They're still in school, weirdo," my sister chimes in.

That's when I realize it's only two-thirty. "Ugh… I don't know why I thought they were out already." I grab a bottle of water out of the mini-fridge and chug half of it down. "Well, give them kisses from their favorite auntie."

They both kiss me goodbye, and I don't miss the way Joaquin grabs my sister's hand and brings it to his lips, kissing it before wrapping his arm around her waist. I sigh. I want to be jealous, but after Sam nearly destroyed her and abandoned Iris, I'm so ecstatic that she has Joaquin who constantly showers both of his girls in love.

I pull my phone out, and like a creep, I get on Colton's social media and try to see if there are any pictures of him and the girl, but the only one I see is one he's tagged in, posing with a girl at what looks like a club.

I toss my phone down, pop a piece of gum in my mouth, and head out to finish the tattoo.

It's my turn to close, so by the time I have everything wiped down I'm exhausted. I set the alarm and lock up, and with my pepper spray out, I hustle to my car. By the time I make it into my apartment twenty minutes later, I just want to hit the hay.

In the bathroom, I quickly brush out my refreshed cotton candy pink hair and pile it up on my head. I moisturize after washing my makeup off. Once my teeth are brushed, I head into my bedroom, crawl onto my bed, and collapse face first.

Thankfully, I'm exhausted and it doesn't take long to fall asleep.

eight

COLTON

My feet slap against the track at the high school. I've come to practice with the varsity team, and now we're finishing up, running laps. Some of these kids have the talent and are already set to attend Big 10 schools.

These guys definitely give me a run for my money as we race around the track. I'm honestly in the best shape of my life, and these kids are pushing me to go faster and faster.

We slow to a jog, me pounding the players' fists as they run past me toward the locker room.

They shout as they run past, "Great playing with you, Colton."

"Thanks for the shirts."

I grab my water and take a generous a drink and then grab my towel, wiping my face off. Coach Morrison, who was my coach, comes walking toward me. "Son, I believe you're in even better shape than I remember. Have you been approached by the NFL?"

I shake my head. "Nah, I missed my shot, but I appreciate it." I change the subject. "It sounds like you guys are already raising lots of money for the fundraiser."

"Yeah, I still can't thank you and the Fire for everything you guys have done." We stop outside the doors to the locker room. "Anytime you want to come workout, talk, or whatever with the team, the door is always open to you."

I take his offered hand. "I appreciate it, and always happy to help. You made me the player I am today." I pull him toward me into the half handshake, half hug.

"Thank you, Colton." He slaps me on my shoulder.

I grab my bag and trek across the field to the parking lot.

"Colton." I hear my name being yelled and turn to see Leesa jogging across the field toward me. "Hey, I'm glad I caught you. Blake wanted me to ask you if you want to meet us and some of our friends for drinks tonight."

Blake is her boyfriend. He's a cool guy, and they're very much together. She has no interest in anything other than friendship with me. I've been trying to branch out, meet new people.

"Yeah, that sounds like fun. Text me the place and time."

We say our goodbyes, and I climb in my SUV and make my way to my place. I'm in desperate need of a shower and something to eat—maybe even a nap.

I step into Blackjack's Bar and Grill spotting Leesa and Blake with several other people. She sees me and waves me over. Blake and I exchange handshakes, and Leesa smiles up at me. "We're so glad you came. Come meet everyone." By everyone she means her sister, and that's when I realize this was a set up.

"Layla, come meet Colton." A girl with auburn hair comes over, smiling nervously. "Colton, this is my sister Layla."

I hold my hand out. "Nice meeting you." I don't want to be rude, but I really want to walk out of here and go home.

Leesa looks between the two of us and smiles. "I'll just be over here." She signals to another couple who just walked up.

I turn back to Layla, and she shakes her head. "Sorry about this. I just ended a five-year relationship, and she thinks I need to get back on the horse." She sighs. "I'm not ready to date."

I can't help but let out a sigh of relief. "Honestly, that is great because I'm in love with someone and not ready to give up on her yet."

I've had a lot of time to think about everything, and I know it's selfish, but I want her. I'll always want her. I'm giving her space right now, but not for long. There will never be anyone else for me, and I know she feels the same way. Heidi is hurt and scared, but if she lets me, I'll prove to her that she can trust her heart with me again.

"Cool, how about I buy you a drink and pretend to flirt, and then later I'll tell my sister you weren't my type."

I laugh. "That sounds good." With a hand on the small of her back, I lead her to the bar, and she buys me a beer.

"So, tell me about this girl," Layla says before taking a drink of her beer.

She listens as I tell her anything. I know I don't know her, but maybe that's why it's so much easier to tell her. When I finish, which is up to the night at the tattoo studio, I drink the last of my beer down. "And that's, that."

"Wow, I mean, I get why she'd be hurt, I do, but I also get why you did it." She signals to the bartender to grab her another drink. Layla then turns back to me and looks over my shoulder. "Umm... Does Heidi have pink hair?"

"Yeah, why?"

She leans in. "She's here and she's looking your way."

I set my beer down and look behind me; sure enough, there she is. She's with her brother and her sister Greta.

Heidi gets up from the table and moves through the bar, heading toward the front door. I chase after her and stop her in the middle of the parking lot. "Don't touch me." She hisses, wrenching her arm out of my grip.

"That was nothing in there. Just a friend trying to fix me up, but that's not what I want." I lean down so I'm in her face. "I want you—I want you, and I know I hurt you, but I thought I was doing the right thing."

"Everything okay?" I know it's Miles who just walked out. "Heidi?"

She's staring at me when she answers him. "I-I'm fine, Miles. You can go." I want to do a fist pump, but she'd probably kick me in the balls.

"Okay, I'm a phone call away, and I don't mind getting arrested for assault." I feel his eyes on me, and I don't blame him for threatening me—he's always looked out for his sisters. He leans in and says, "Remember—I know how to bury a body and not get caught." Miles chuckles as he walks away.

"Please come home with me. Let's talk. If you want things to be over, then I'll respect your wishes."

I feel like it takes forever before she finally gives me a nod, but for the first time ever, I feel hopeful. I hold my hand out to her, and when she slides hers into mine, I lead her over to my SUV and open the passenger door for her.

The moment she's inside, I shut the door. I feel her eyes on me as I make my way around the front and then climb in. Her floral scent surrounds me, and all I want to do is pull her into my arms and kiss her until she's breathless.

Instead, I start my car and then pull out of the parking lot. The radio plays quietly, filling the awkward silence. I hate it. We used to be able to talk about anything, but now it's weird. It's only temporary, I hope.

We pull into my driveway, and I park. "Wait for me," I tell her as I hop out. As I round the front, she's hopping out.

"You're not the boss of me." She huffs and stomps around me, heading up the walkway to the front door.

I cough to cover the laugh that threatens to bubble up. She would get sassy with me when we were younger, and I'd spank her ass. Heidi *loved* getting spanked, and I loved doing it. She's the only one I've ever played with like that and the only one I ever will.

Not like there has been a ton of women since her, seeing how for two years I was fighting cancer.

I pull my keys out of my pocket and step past her to unlock the front door. I hold it open as Heidi walks in. I shut the door behind her. "Do you want something to drink?"

She nods. "Yeah, thanks."

Heidi follows me into the kitchen and sits at the breakfast bar. I grab two beers out of the fridge and hand her one. She pops the tab and takes a drink before setting it down.

"I'm sorry about what I said the night you came to see me at the studio." She picks up the can again, tipping it back, and slugging it down. "I saw you with a girl at the sandwich shop. I hid behind a plant because I didn't want you to see me. My heart felt like it was breaking all over again."

"She's just my friend—Leesa has a serious boyfriend and is not interested. I'm doing some charity work for the high school football team, and she's helping. Tonight, she wanted to hook me up with her sister, but neither of us were looking for that; at least, with each other." I step toward her, stopping an arm's length away. "Thank you for saying sorry."

"Where do we go from here?" Heidi stares up at me, and before I can stop myself, I reach out and stroke her cheek.

"I don't know, baby." I try to hide the hope I feel, but it's useless. "What if we start over? Maybe we could date? Maybe we get to know each other again."

Heidi bites her lower lip. "What if things aren't the same anymore between us?" she asks, softly.

"Then at least we can say we tried."

She doesn't answer right away, and I start to get nervous, but thankfully when she answers it makes me smile. "Okay, let's date, but promise me we'll take it slow."

I lean down so we're eye to eye. "Baby, I promise we'll take it as fast or as slow as you want to take it."

She surprises me by wrapping her arms around me and hugging me tight. I return it and place my lips against her temple.

"Will you stay with me tonight? I swear, no funny business. I just want to hold you."

nine

HEIDI

I should say no. I should tell Colton to take me home, but I don't. I nod and then take his hand. He leads me into his bedroom and grabs me a t-shirt out of his dresser. "You can wear this. I'll get you a toothbrush."

He disappears into the bathroom, and a minute later he comes walking back out. "You are all set." I walk into the bathroom and find the t-shirt and toothbrush sitting on the counter.

I pull the rubber band from around my wrist and put my hair into a knot on top of my head. I open his medicine cabinet and smile. When we were fifteen, he had an issue with acne. His mom took him to a dermatologist who set him up with a skin care line, and I'm not surprised he still uses it today.

Of course, he has great freaking skin. I use his stuff to wash my face and then moisturize. I open the toothbrush and make quick work of brushing my teeth. Once I finish, I take off my clothes, including my bra, and throw his t-shirt on. It hits me mid-thigh and reminds me of when we were younger, and I would wear his clothes.

I grab the material, bringing it to my nose and inhaling his scent. God, what am I doing? I let it go and take the rubber band out of my hair, shaking it out. I step back into Colton's bedroom and find him lying in bed. He's shirtless, and the sheet is pulled up to his waist.

I ignore the way my mouth waters as I walk around to the other side, quickly sliding under the covers. He reaches over me and turns the lamp off. His touch causes me to do a full-body shiver—fuck, this was a mistake. I should have told him to take me home.

Once the room is bathed in darkness, he grabs me and positions me half on and half off him. His heart pounds in his chest, and before I can think better of it, I kiss him right over it.

"This was a dumb idea," Colton mutters from next to me. For a second, I think he's talking about us dating, but then he starts talking again. "My cock is so hard right now, and I promised you there would be no funny business."

I don't say anything as I let my hand slide down his chest, until I reach his hard cock, testing the strength of the stitching of his boxer briefs. It jerks from my touch, but instead of letting things go further, he grabs my hand and brings it up to his chest.

"Don't you want to have sex?" I try to read the expression on his face, but it's difficult in the dark. "You're hard."

"I know, and I'd love nothing more than to be with you, but I promised you no funny business, and I meant it."

I lay my head on his chest, listening to the steady beat of his heart. It doesn't take long until I feel sleep pull me under.

I'm not sure what time it is, but I know it's still nighttime. I reach out and find Colton's side of the bed empty. A sound comes from the bathroom, and it causes me to climb out of bed.

A noise that sounds like a moan hits my ears the closer I get to the closed door. I lean in and place my ear to it. It takes a second to realize what I'm listening to—Colton is jerking off, and why does that turn me on?

"Oh fuck, Heidi," he whispers, and I turn, leaning against the wall next to the door.

I pull up his t-shirt and slide my hand into my panties. My clit is throbbing, and I'm wet already. I rub my clit as I listen to him jerk his cock, thinking of me. I imagine that I'm in there, and he's fucking me.

We learned so much about our bodies together. Once we broke the seal, we were like rabbits, taking every chance we could to be together.

I focus on the task at hand and rub my clit as I listen to his moans. If I close my eyes, I can picture his powerful body as he jerks his cock. In no time I begin to come, biting my lip to keep from crying out.

His groan signals his orgasm as well, and I hustle back to his bed, jumping in. I lay on my side, pretending to be asleep. A few minutes later he tiptoes silently into the bedroom and slides into the bed.

I try to keep myself completely relaxed, and he fits himself to my back, wrapping his arm around me. "I love you, Heidi," he whispers against my neck.

It isn't long before he's snoring softly, and I thankfully follow behind him a short while later.

It has been a week since Colton and I decided to start dating again. I assumed we would start with maybe a coffee date or lunch. Instead, Colton has basically been living at mine and Greta's apartment.

He showed up with groceries and a suitcase, scoring the spare key from my traitor sister. Every morning he's made breakfast for me and Greta. He then would leave and go practice or workout. After, he would come back, and make me lunch before I'd go to the studio, and if I was already gone he'd bring me lunch there.

I drew the line at dinner. I didn't want him to think he had to do things for me because of what happened.

"That's not why I'm doing this." He crossed his arms over his chest.

I shook my head. "Then why?"

"Because I love you, and I want to take care of you."

I almost melted into a puddle right there in front of him. Instead, I stepped toward him and pushed up on my toes. I kissed him softly on the lips and then stepped back. "Well, tonight dinner is on me." I told him. "I'll make you my mom's homemade fried chicken."

Every year for his birthday, my mom would make him her fried chicken and scalloped potatoes. It was always his favorite meal.

"That's a deal." He winked and then walked to the door of my apartment. "I'll see you later." Colton opened the door, but instead of walking out of it, he turned back to me.

In a flash he was on me, his lips on mine. I opened my mouth to his tongue, and suddenly I was thrust back to when we learned how to French kiss. It was so wet and awkward, but we practiced every chance we got—until we got very, very good at it.

Our kiss ended far too soon, but we were taking things slow. Hell, we've slept in the same bed and have managed not to have sex. It's getting hard to resist him, though. He's so handsome and has a way of peering into my soul.

Now I focus make on the chicken frying on the stove.

"That smells delicious." Colton comes up behind me and places his large hands on my waist. He leans down and places a kiss on the side of my neck.

"Thanks, I hope it tastes good." I turn my head to smile up at him. "How was practice?"

"Good. I'm ready for the playoffs to begin. The first game is away, and then the second is home. That's, of course, if we win the first game." He takes a drink of his water. "It was so great when I was able to start playing football again."

My eyes burn now that I know the reason he hadn't played until last year. There are still so many questions I want to ask but have been afraid to. Now just doesn't seem to be the right time to ask them, so I'll wait. "I'm sure it was. You're even better than I remember."

"Thanks. I trained hard to get back in shape, and I even worked with a trainer who specializes in football.

It took some time for my skills to come back, but when it did, I was relieved. I was afraid I'd lost it forever."

It suddenly feels like there are rocks in my gut. I focus on the chicken when I think about all he went through without me. His choice—no, I'm not going there. If we're going to date, I can't hold that over his head.

I also need to tell him about the child we lost; he deserves to know. "Ahem... You could never lose that kind of gift. You were born to play football," I say quietly.

He moves in close, the heat from his body seeping into me. My breathing picks up speed, and I bite my lip to keep from moaning.

Colton's arms slide around my waist, and goose bumps pop up all over my body. I feel his lips touch my ear and quiver with pleasure. "Thank you for saying that." He places his lips against my temple, kissing me softly.

I shake my head. "I speak the truth." He was the starting varsity quarterback from our sophomore year to our senior year. Everyone thought he'd go pro, but then he disappeared. "I always loved watching you play."

After the games, before he'd head into the locker rooms, he'd run over to where I was sitting, and jump up as I leaned down until our lips met. Our picture was in the front of the yearbook our senior year. The picture is also in a frame that's in a box, under my bed.

"Now leave me alone so I can finish cooking." I bump him back with my butt.

He chuckles and then pulls a stool out at his kitchen counter. I feel Colton's eyes on me as I move around his kitchen as I finish up dinner.

ten

COLTON

It's still dark when my alarm goes off. I ease out of bed and stumble toward the bathroom. I'm meeting Tyrell at the gym to get a workout in before practice. After using the bathroom, I wash my face and brush my teeth.

I slip on some basketball shorts and t-shirt. I step around the bed until I'm on Heidi's side. I sit next to her hip and brush her cotton candy pink hair out of her face.

She's so fucking pretty, she takes my breath away. Her eyelids flutter open, and she pushes up, smiling at me with her sleepy grin. "Hi," she whispers.

"Hey, I'm going to go meet Ty to work out. I didn't want you to wake up and not know where I went." I lean down and kiss her softly on the lips. "I'll be back before you head to the studio."

"'Kay," Heidi whispers and then lays her head down. "Love you." She closes her eyes and starts snoring softly.

"I love you too," I whisper, even though I know she can't hear me.

The sky is that dark inky blue. Traffic is light, but in thirty minutes or so it'll start picking up. I reach the gym and park next to Ty's minivan. I can't help it and chuckle as he climbs out.

"Stop laughing, motherfucker. I make that shit look good." He turns, twerking at me, and I kick him in the ass.

I jog away from him, laughing as he throws his duffle bag at me. We head into the locker room. "How are things with Heidi?"

I smile as I tuck my bag into my locker. "Great, we're taking it slow—slower than I want—

but I'm afraid if I push too hard she'll run."

"I'm happy for you, brother. Moni will want to meet her and give her approval."

"Sure thing, man. You set it up, and we'll be there."

We both slam our lockers shut and head out to start lifting.

Heidi holds my hand as we walk through the grocery store. I talked her into making her mom's famous chocolate chip cookies, and in my other hand is the basket with everything we need.

It's becoming harder and harder to keep myself in check around her. Every morning I wake up with a hard-on and her wrapped around me like a spider monkey. Don't get me wrong, I love it, but she rubs against my dick, making it ache, and I can't do what I want—strip her bare and thrust my cock inside her.

We kiss and cuddle, but we haven't taken it any further. I'm letting her set the pace with the physical stuff. I know I'm lucky she's even giving this a shot. I keep hold of her hand as we wait in line to check out.

I bring her hand to my lips, kissing the back of it. Heidi smiles up at me and bites her lip before turning away. We get to the checkout, and I let go to pay for the groceries. She grabs the bags.

"My parents want to see you." They always adored Heidi, and they were so pissed at me about my decision to break things off. When I called Mom to tell her that Heidi was giving me a shot, she'd started crying—she was beyond happy.

"I'd love to see them," she says as we step outside.

They moved home last week—I'm their only child and Mom doesn't like being far away. We reach my SUV and I take the bags, loading them into the back. "They're staying in a rental right now, but once they're settled, we'll set something up." I kiss Heidi before helping her inside, shutting the door behind her. I climb in the driver's side and we head home.

Back at my place I follow Heidi into the kitchen to watch her start baking. She looks perfect in my kitchen, and it feels right that she's here. My heart clenches in my chest because I could've had this— had her for the past five years. I can almost imagine our kids running around. We'd probably have a dog or two, maybe a pet rabbit.

"Colton?" I blink and find Heidi standing in front of me. "Are you okay?"

I shake my head. "I-I." I grab her hands. "Can I show you something?"

Heidi reaches up, cupping my face. "You can show me anything." I lean down and kiss her softly.

"I'll be right back." I head into my bedroom and grab the journal out of my closet. It's not a journal like one might think, but if I made it and beat cancer, I wanted to get my experience on paper so I wouldn't forget, and if I ever saw Heidi again, I wanted her to see it that way she'd understand why I left her.

I find her sitting at the breakfast bar. I take the seat beside her. "I want to tell you about everything with the cancer."

"Okay." Heidi gives me a soft smile.

She opens the book and reads the first page. "I was so angry when I found out about the cancer. All I wanted was to marry you and play pro-ball. Mom immediately made me talk to someone. And he suggested writing down my thoughts."

I don't take my eyes off her as she reads the first few pages. Her tears drip down her cheeks, and a whimper slips past her lips when she lands on the picture from my first day of chemo.

My shirt is off, and the port I had placed is there for her to see. Heidi spends the next half hour reading each entry and staring at each picture. I hold her why she sobs at the picture of my dad shaving my head.

I hand Heidi a tissue when she gets to the last picture of me ringing the bell on the day of my last chemo treatment. She closes the book and doesn't say anything. I watch her stand and let herself out of my backdoor.

"Fuck," I whisper to myself. Maybe it was too much, too soon.

I open the door and spot her sitting at the stop of the steps. Her forehead rests on her knees, her cries soft and heartbreaking. I move across the deck and sit behind her, my legs snug against hers.

Heidi leans back against my chest. I wrap my arms around her, hugging her tight as she cries into my shirt.

"Baby, no more tears. I'm fine, I'm healthy, and I'm in remission."

She shakes her head. "I know, but fuck… I'm mad at you. I would've helped you, taken care of you, and I hate the thought of you suffering alone."

I kiss Heidi's forehead. "Baby, I fucked up—I know I did, and I'm so sorry."

We stay where we are until her tears dry up. I help her stand and lead her into the house a while later. "I'll be back in a minute." I watch her walk into the hallway and hear the "snick" of the bathroom door shutting.

"Fuck," I whisper.

A moment later I hear her footsteps. She rounds the corner and comes toward me, wrapping her arms around my waist. I wrap her in a hug, kissing her forehead.

"Ow, shit." I jump as Heidi pinches my side and then slaps my arm. "What was that for?"

"Don't ever leave me like that again. We're a team! If there is something to fight—we fight together." She steps back and then pushes me. "Jerk-wad."

I grab her and throw her over my shoulder, slapping her ass twice. "I see we're still sassy as ever." Heidi slides down my body until we're eye to eye, her legs are wrapped around my hips. "Baby, I promise you we'll fight whatever comes our way."

"Pinky swear?" She holds up her pinky finger.

I do the same, saying, "Pinky swear," and then wrap mine around hers.

Heidi's eyes go soft and then heated. "Take me to bed, Colton."

I freeze. "Are you sure?" I, of course, want that more than anything, but I need her to initiate it.

She gives me a smile and then nods. "I've never been surer."

That's all I need before I'm attacking her lips, forcing her mouth open with mine, and dipping my tongue inside. Heidi moans into my mouth the moment my tongue brushes against hers.

I move blindly through my house until I'm in my bedroom. She clings to me like a spider monkey as I climb onto my bed and lay her down so I can pull away to look at her. She's a fucking vision with her cotton candy-colored hair spread across my pillows. Her lips are swollen from my kisses.

I grab the hem of her shirt and pull it up and off. The last time I saw her naked I didn't get to truly admire her beautiful ink. It's all shades of pink and feminine, all Heidi, but my eyes catch the tattoo right over her heart. *"Love doesn't live here anymore"* is written in beautiful scrawl.

Pain hits me right in the chest. It takes her a second to realize that I'm looking at her tattoo. I close my eyes as shame fills me—I caused that pain, a pain that she went and had permanently marked on her skin.

Heidi grabs my face, and I open my eyes. "Whatever is going through your head, stop it." She shakes her head. "It was a mistake. I was hurt and didn't know how to channel it, or how to show it."

I bend down, kissing over her heart and then laying my ear against her chest. Her heart beats wildly as she spears her fingers through my hair. I close my eyes as I listen to the rapid *thump, thump, thump.*

I pull down the cup of her bra, exposing her pink nipple. Heidi's breath catches in her throat as I trace my finger around it, until it hardens. She shows me what she wants when she arches her back, thrusting her nipple into the air.

With a quick maneuver, I'm up and over her with her wrists shackled in one of my hands above her head. I use the other one to pull down the other cup of her bra, and I lean down, licking around the nipple until it hardens too.

Heidi squirms under me, thrusting her pussy against my cock. "Stop teasing me," she moans.

I remember when we were younger, I could make her come with just my mouth wrapped around her nipple. I suck her nipple into my mouth, and with each pull she grips my head and moans.

I rub my hard dick against her, listening to the sounds of her moans when I hit her clit through her shorts. Heidi rocks against me and starts making noises that always let me know she is ready to come.

I switch breasts and suck the other nipple into my mouth. The moment I nip the hardened tip, Heidi's neck is arched back, and her mouth opens in a wordless cry. I shove my hand down her shorts and into her panties. Her cum covers my digits as I rub them up and down her pussy.

Once my fingers are covered, I pull them out of her bottoms, and while she watches me, I bring them to my lips, sucking them inside.

eleven

HEIDI

My pussy spasms as I watch him lick his fingers clean. I grab his wrist and pull on it. He can read what I want because I pull his fingers from his mouth and bring them to my lips.

I moan as I suck his wet digits into my mouth. Colton watches me as I lick his finger, like I'm licking his cock. With his free hand he yanks my bottoms down, and I help while sucking on his fingers.

I let go of his wrist and reach between us, freeing him from his shorts. In seconds he's buried to the hilt inside me. We groan together as he begins to pound into me at a punishing pace.

No one since Colton has been able to make me feel the way that he does. Maybe because we learned so much together. We did a *whole* lot of learning together. He grabs my hands, shackling them in his large grip. His free hand grabs my breast, and he leans down, sucking my nipple into his mouth.

God, he totally remembers how sensitive they are. In no time I'm coming with a sharp cry. Colton moves faster, harder, and his thrusts become erratic. He comes, groaning against my throat.

I feel every hot blast of his cum and know that he came inside me, again, but I can't bring myself to care. He pants against my neck, and I wrap my legs around his and hug him.

He places a kiss behind my ear and then kisses my lips. I smile and reach up, brushing his hair back. Colton pulls his softening cock out of me, and I don't miss our combined arousal as it slides down the crack of my ass.

"I'll be right back." He kisses my lips before sliding off the bed.

He tucks himself into his shorts and then walks into his bathroom. Colton returns with a washcloth in his hand. He quickly cleans me up and then crawls back into bed.

"Want to go have dinner?"

I nod as my stomach growls loudly. I giggle like a stupid schoolgirl, but I can't help it. I'm so fucking happy right now. "The cookie dough is probably ruined."

"That's okay; we can make more tonight." He kisses me and then pulls me out of bed. Colton grabs my clothes, dressing me, and it feels so intimate.

We head into the kitchen where I throw out the cookie dough that I'd managed to mix up before things got intense, and we'd forgotten about it. Luckily, we bought enough ingredients to make lots.

We end up spending the rest of the evening ordering out Chinese and then baking cookies together. Colton and I end our night wrapped naked around each other.

Colton is away for round two of the playoffs—he thought he was going to be home for that game, but it was away. They won the week before and it was an away game. The place was electric as he threw pass after pass. I've never seen him play so well. I'd like to think it was because I was there cheering him on.

Since we all travelled to Chicago to root him on, we sat down close to the field. By the end of the game my voice was hoarse from screaming so loud. I ran onto the field and right into his open arms after the final second of the game, and our picture was in the paper the next day.

The night they won I'd forgotten how pumped Colton could get and how ravenous he was. We'd fucked all over our hotel suite: in the living room, the kitchenette, the hallway, the shower, and finally passed out in the bedroom sprawled.

I was sore for two days afterward, but it was so worth it.

Now I'm working on one of my client's back tattoos. She brought in her own design, a pair of fairy wings. We worked together to tweak the design to make it absolutely perfect.

It takes four hours to do the outline. She'll come back in four weeks, and we'll finish it. Once I wipe it off, I take her over to the mirror to look at it. I know she loves it when she squeals.

I grab my phone, taking pictures of it, and then I send her to the desk where Greta will take her payment. In the office, I grab my phone and quickly check the Atlanta Fire's website. I see that there is seven minutes left, and they're tied with Dallas.

I watch the highlights from the first half and smile. God, Colton is amazingly talented. He should be playing pro-ball, and maybe it'll happen. I've read that it has and if it's going to happen to anyone, I can't think of someone who deserves it more.

"Hey." I turn to find Sierra standing in the doorway. "Nick texted me that Colton is playing phenomenally today." She rubs a hand over her belly, that is massive.

"Yeah, I wish I was there. Regardless, if they win or not, he'll be home tomorrow. What about Nick?" He hasn't traveled much since the incident with the cheerleader.

"He'll be taking the jet home in the morning. He's not a big fan of leaving us for long." I'm so happy my sister has found a man who loves her the way Nick does. The fact that he's embraced impending fatherhood with gusto has made all of us love the crude, loveable giant more.

I wrap my arms around my sister, kissing her cheek. "I love you, sissy." I bend down. "I love you, my sweet little niece. Poor Max is going to be outnumbered." So far, he's the only boy.

"Well, you never know what will happen down the road." I leave her to go set up my station for my next client, but my mind is on the baby Colton and I lost. I feel like it was a boy, but I push those thoughts away like I always do.

I've yet to tell Colton, I'm afraid it'll break him to know the truth. He'll blame himself and it isn't his fault, any more than it was mine. I've had five years to accept that, and I know it will take time for him. I just have to tell him first.

I feel the bed shift and freeze, until I realize it's Colton. He rolls me to my back and settles between my legs. I reach up in the dark, grabbing his face. "I'm sorry," is all I say before I pull his lips down to mine.

I can feel that he needs this, and I let him use me. Over and over he fucks me with abandon. By the time either of us falls asleep the sun is starting to rise.

Colton doesn't move as I slip out of bed. It's noon, and since we slept through breakfast, I decide to make him lunch in bed. I slip his t-shirt on over my head and pad into the bathroom.

I tie my hair up into a bun as I head out to the kitchen. Grilled cheese sounds good, so I grab the griddle, bread, butter, and cheese. I make two for him and only one for me. I spoon some fruit and potato chips onto our plates.

I carry the plates into the bedroom where Colton is sleeping, facedown and naked. Fuck, he's the perfect male specimen. I set the plates down and climb onto the bed. I kiss each ass cheek and work my way up his back.

"Eeek..." I shriek as Colton flips us, maneuvering us until I'm on my back and he's between my legs. His cock is hard, resting against my pussy. I shake my head. "No way, mister. My vagina needs a break from little Colton."

"Little?"

I giggle. "I'm sorry, I meant big ol' Colton."

His eyes soften as he smiles down at me. Colton leans down, kissing me softly on the lips.

"I'm sorry the team lost. It sounded like you put up a helluva fight." I reach up, kissing him on the lips.

He kisses me back before leaning down, kissing my neck. "Thanks, baby. I'm disappointed, but we put up a fight until the end. My parents will be here later this afternoon."

"I can't wait to see them. I'm glad they were there since I couldn't be. You play better than you did in high school, and you were phenomenal back then."

"You are going to give me a big head."

"I like your big head," I say saucily.

Colton kisses me deep and hard and then pulls back. "I'll be right back." He hops up, and I watch him disappear into the bathroom. He's in there for a few minutes before he comes back out, and I take in his male beauty.

He throws some ratty old sweats on and then climbs into bed with me. I grab his plate and hand it to him. We snuggle and eat, feeding each other off our plates. Colton takes our plates into the kitchen while I strip out of his t-shirt and walk naked into his bathroom. I climb into the shower. The warm water sluices down my body, and I smile as two strong arms wrap around me.

His cock is hard, pressed against the small of my back. "Don't even think about it." I turn in Colton's arms, smiling up at him. "We don't have time."

He sticks his bottom lip out, like a child pouting. A giggle erupts from my throat. I grab the body wash and squeeze a large dollop into my hand. I hold Colton's gaze as I start rubbing my soap covered hands all over his muscled chest.

He bites his lip as my hands glide down his stomach, tracing the V. I hold his gaze as I squat down to wash his legs, trying very hard to ignore the fact that his cock is right in my face.

It's long, thick, and so freaking hard—no wonder I'm so sore. I wag my finger at it. "No... I can't. I'm sore."

Colton's chuckle makes me smile up at him. "Get up here, cock tease." I stand and he runs his soapy hands along my body. My nipples harden as he runs his hands all over my breasts. "See, it's not very nice to be teased, is it?" he whispers.

twelve

HEIDI

We managed to finish our shower without having sex, but it was very, *very* hard to say no to him. He can be very convincing and looks too darn cute when he pouts. Don't get me wrong, I'm *always* very willing when it comes to sex with him. I just like to make him work for it.

Colton is out in the living room, while I put the finishing touches on my hair—I kept it down and added beach waves to it. I'm wearing a white tank top and a pink paisley skirt that hits me mid-thigh.

What will his mom say about my tattoos? My pink hair? Cari and Jim have always treated me like their daughter, but I was different back then. I step out of the bedroom and find Colton sitting on the sofa, and he stands when he sees me. "Fuck, you're gorgeous."

He's in a faded blue Nike t-shirt and gray khaki style shorts that show off his amazing ass. His blond hair is still wet and combed straight back. Colton's feet are bare, and he has pretty feet for a guy.

"You're not so bad yourself," I say as he comes toward me. Once he's close enough, I grab his shirt and pull him to me. I wrap my arms around his waist and squeeze him tight.

I hear car doors slam and smile widely up at Colton before I run for the door. Cari sees me and screams before we run to each other. The moment her arms are around me I begin to sob uncontrollably, and she does the same.

"Oh, sweet girl, I've missed you." She hugs me tight. "I'm so, so sorry. We tried to talk him out of it," Cari whispers quietly.

"It's okay." I sniffle.

"No, sweet girl, it's not, but thank you for saying that."

I'm pulled away from Cari, smiling up at Jim. "She can't hog you, darlin'."

I smile up at the man who was a second dad to me. "Hey, Jim." I wrap my arms around him.

"Guys, let's head inside." Colton takes me from his dad and wraps his arm around my shoulders. The four of us head inside, and while Colton and his dad get us drinks, Cari grabs my arms. "Your ink is beautiful. Did one of your sisters do it for you?"

I nod, smiling. "Sierra did both of my arms. Mona did this one." I stand and show Cari the back of my calf; it's four female sugar skulls and one male. "It symbolizes the five of us."

"You girls were always so artistic. I'm so proud of you." She pulls me into a hug. Cari grabs a light pink lock. "So pretty. It's nice to see you haven't lost your love for the color pink." She wraps her arms around me again.

"It is definitely still my favorite color." I grab my phone and pull up pictures. I show her pictures of Iris, and tell her about Max, Juaquin, and Nick. She listens and smiles while I tell her stories about each picture.

"My gosh, the last time I saw Iris it was her second birthday. She looks just like Mona, and he's such a handsome little guy. It is so wonderful everyone is doing well." She's quiet for a minute. "Would you ask your mom if it is okay if I reach out?"

When Colton and his parents left my life, it hurt my parents too; they were always close with Cari and Jim. "I will, I promise."

Colton and Jim join us, my man taking a seat next to me. He and his dad start talking about the football season. I've always loved watching Colton play, but I know the bare minimum about football.

Once we're finished with our drinks, we head out to have dinner at Nick's restaurant, *Nicholas*.

I practically sprint down the hallway of the mother/baby unit, anxious to get to my sister and my new niece. I turn to wait for Colton who is shaking his head and chuckling as he walks toward me. "Sorry," I say and shrug.

"Don't be sorry. I know you're excited." He wraps his arm around my shoulders, hugging me into his side. I sigh happily as he kisses my temple.

We reach their room, and I knock rapidly on the door and then open it. Sierra is sitting crisscross applesauce with a swaddled bundle in her arms. "Hey, Momma," I whisper to her as I move to the side of the bed.

I hug her and kiss her cheek and then take my niece from her mom. "Hi, Ember. I'm your aunt Heidi." I bend down and kiss her forehead. She makes a squeaky noise and then continues to snooze.

Colton hugs and kisses Sierra before coming over to me. He strokes a hand over Ember's soft dark blonde hair.

The door opens, and Nick walks in with a bag. "Hey, you two," he says, coming to me and kissing me on top of the head. He leans down and kisses the baby before going to Sierra. They share a kiss that has Colton and me turning away from them.

I hand the sleeping baby over to Colton. She looks so tiny in his big, strong arms. A pain hits me in the chest so hard it knocks the breath out of me. My stomach turns, and my eyes burn. Our child would have been four; no doubt they'd be spoiled by their family.

I escape out into the hall, taking a deep breath. The door opens, and I turn, expecting to find Colton there, but instead it's my sister.

"Sorry," I say quietly.

Sierra shakes her head. "Don't be sorry. I'm so sorry, sweetheart."

"No, stop. This is your day. I'll be okay." I take a deep breath, wrap my arm around Sierra's waist, and lead her back inside their room. Nick sits on the side of the bed with their daughter in his arms.

Colton leans down when I reach his side. "You okay?"

I smile up at him. "Yeah, I just got hot for a minute."

He looks at me in a way that proves he doesn't believe me, but he lets me be for now.

The minute I open the door I can smell the scent of spaghetti sauce. "Lucy, I'm home," I holler, doing a terrible Ricky Ricardo impression. I step into the apartment, shutting the door behind me, and go in search of Greta.

I find my sister in the kitchen stirring something in a big pot. "Hey, girlie," she says and then comes toward me and throws her arms around me. "I've missed you."

"I know. I'm sorry I've been gone so much."

"Don't apologize. I'm happy for you and Colton. I still can't believe he was ever sick." My stomach turns just thinking about it. "Shit, forget I just said that."

I grab a Coke Zero out of the fridge. "Seriously, it's okay. I forgave him. We talked and worked things out." Greta doesn't know that I'd lost a baby either. "I'm happy, Greta, but I'm also scared to death. What if he gets sick again, but this time I lose him forever?"

Greta places her hands on my shoulders. "I doubt that is going to happen, but with you fighting at his side, I'm sure he can beat anything."

I pull her into a hug. "Thanks. Now feed me."

We spend the evening, eating together, and then we cuddle up on the sofa and watch a marathon of Hell's Kitchen.

I sit on the side of the bed a few hours later and pull up my text messages.

| **Heidi:** | Hey, just wanted to tell you goodnight. |

I set my phone on the nightstand and strip out of my close, changing into one of my light pink spaghetti strap nightgowns. I quickly tie up my hair in high ponytail. After washing my face and brushing my teeth, I crawl into my bed.

I grab my phone and see Colton texted me back.

| **Colton:** | Hey, baby, I miss you. I don't like going to bed without you. |
| **Heidi:** | I think you'll survive one night without me. You survived five years without me. |

The moment I hit send, I instantly regret it. Fuck, I so didn't mean that.

| **Heidi:** | Oh God, Colton, I'm so sorry. That was a shitty thing to say. |

I quickly dial him, but it goes right to voicemail. "Colton, I'm so sorry. That was such a snarky thing to say, and I swear that wasn't the way I meant it. I- I'm coming over."

I hang up and grab some shorts and slip them on. My phone pings, and I quickly pick it up.

| **Colton:** | I know you didn't. Just so you know I was alive, but I wasn't living. I couldn't live without you. Goodnight, and we'll talk tomorrow. |

Heidi: I wasn't living without you either. I want to see you; can I come over?

I sit on the side of the bed and wait for him to answer. After an hour, it's clear he's not going to respond. I lie down, but it's a long time before I find sleep.

thirteen

COLTON

I jog along the bike path, my mind wandering, and an ache fills my gut. I'm not mad at Heidi; I know she wasn't trying to be hurtful. The truth of the matter is there is a lot truth to what she said.

It was all my fault—all of it. Last night I just needed to wallow in self-pity. I had a fitful night of sleep. When I get back to my SUV I use my towel in the back to wipe the sweat from my face.

I climb into my SUV and crank the air to cool me off. I decide to go home and shower first, then I'll go find Heidi. When I reach the end of my street I find her car in my driveway. I pull in and spot her sitting on the front steps.

I jump out and watch her stand as I walk up the sidewalk. She doesn't say anything, just walks right up to me and wraps her arms around my waist. I wrap mine around her shoulders and place my lips against her temple.

"Sorry I went silent last night," I say quietly. "I was having a pity party because you're right. I lost five years."

Heidi shocks me when she covers my mouth with her hand. "No more pity party; no more thinking about the past." She cups my face. "I love you, Colton."

"I love you too, baby." I kiss her slowly and thoroughly and then lead her into the house where she helps me shower.

I pull into the parking lot of the Fire's home office. Stan, my coach, called asking me to come to the office for a meeting with him, Nick, and Gordo. Heidi had no clue what the meeting was about, but I didn't really expect her to.

Are they going to let me go since we didn't go all the way? If they are, what will happen to Heidi and me? It's not like I expect her to uproot her life and follow me somewhere else, but am I ready to give up playing?

Fuck, I shake off those thoughts and take a deep breath before I head inside. My dress shoes slap against the granite flooring as I walk down the hallway to Gordo's office.

Nick steps out into the hall, smiling widely when he sees me. "There he is." His big, booming voice bounces down the hall.

I reach him and stick my hand out to shake his, but instead he pulls me into a backslapping hug.

He steps back and smiles like a lunatic. "Come on in." Nick leads me into the office, and Stan and Gordo stand as enter, along with two other men I don't recognize. "Colton, I'd like to introduce you to Tim Michaelson and Carl Jacobs—the recruiter and head coach from the Tennessee Tigers."

What. The. fuck. I take a deep breath and step forward, holding out my hand. I hope to God they can't feel my hand trembling or sweating. "It's nice to meet you both." I remind myself to keep eye contact and keep my grip firm.

"Hi, Colton. Thank you for coming down here to speak to us."

Everyone sits down, and I swear that I blackout.

I pace back and forth as I wait for Heidi to come out. Tonight, I'm taking her to Nick's restaurant, Urban Fusion. After the meeting, I asked him if he could get me a table there.

I want to make this a night to remember. She knows there's some big news that I'm going to share but doesn't know the details. I hear the click, click of Heidi's heels. My mouth drops open as she steps into the living room.

Heidi is wearing a black tank top dress that skims her curves and hits her mid-thigh. On her feet are a pair of pink peep toe pumps that do wonders for her already gorgeous legs.

Her pink hair is down in loose waves, and her makeup is light. "Damn, baby. You are stunning."

Heidi's cheeks turn an adorable shade of pink. "You're not so bad yourself."

I'm still in my suit that I wore to my meeting, sans jacket. "I almost don't want to take you out. I'm going to have to beat the men away from you."

"I only have eyes for you," she says softly.

"Ditto, baby." With a hand to the small of her back, I lead her out to my SUV. I help her in, ignoring the way my dick takes notice of her sexy as fuck body. My hand rests on her thigh as we head to the restaurant.

We're quiet the whole way there, and she rests her hand on top of mine. We reach the restaurant, and I pull up to the valet. I hop out and jog around to Heidi's door and help her out.

I hand the keys to the attendant and then lead my girl inside. The hostess leads us to our table, and I don't miss the way men watch Heidi as we go by. I want to hide her from their prying eyes.

To my surprise the hostess leads us upstairs to a private room. "Dinner is on Mr. Echols tonight." I open my mouth to refuse, but she hands me a card and then leaves us.

"What's that?" Heidi looks at me as I pull out the chair for her.

I take my seat and open the envelope.

Colton,

Dinner is on me tonight, and I won't take no for an answer. So help me God I will sic Sierra on you. My girl is rockin' the new momma hormones, and she'll kick your ass. You deserve this.

I'm so proud of you.

Nick

That means a lot. I've only known Nick a short time, but I have a lot of respect for him. I thought I may have been wrong when the whole Staci thing happened, but that situation worked itself out.

I hand the card to Heidi. She reads it and then smiles at me. "I love that man, but now I'm even more excited to hear your news." Her smile is expectant, and she sets card on the table.

Our waiter interrupts us, setting a bucket with a bottle of champagne down. He pops the cork and pours some into the two flutes he has in his hand. "Courtesy of Mr. Echols. I'll be back soon to take your order."

We thank him, and he disappears. "Okay, you better tell me this news."

I take a deep breath. "I've been invited to the Tennessee Tigers training camp."

At first she's silent, but then she smiles big and wide. "Are you serious? Oh my God, this is amazing."

Heidi gets up from her seat and comes around the table, sitting sideways on my lap. She wraps her arms around me, hugging me tight.

"I'm so proud of you," she whispers against my ear.

I pull back until I can see her beautiful face. "I love you, Heidi."

She grabs my face and leans in, kissing me softly on the lips. "I love you too, baby."

The rest of our evening is amazing. First, we drank the bottle of champagne and then ate some of the most tender steaks either of us have ever eaten. When they brought out the crème brulee, we took turns feeding it to each other.

Since Nick paid for dinner, I left our waiter a hefty tip and then wrapped my arm around my girl's waist as we made our way out of the restaurant. While we waited for valet to bring my SUV, we kissed and stood in the moonlight with our arms around each other.

I pull up to the house and right into the garage. Climbing out, I come around to Heidi's side and help her out. I don't even get the door shut before she's on me, and I'm slamming into the side of my vehicle.

She pulls my mouth down to hers, attacking my lips like she's starving for me. My tongue tangles with hers as I slide my hands down her body until I reach the hem of her dress and move my hands up, taking the dress with them.

Once I have it around her hips, I grab her ass and lift her off the ground. Heidi's legs immediately hug my hips. I spin us so her back is pressed to the side of the SUV.

Heidi pulls her mouth from mine. "I need you." That's all my girl needs to say before I'm ripping her panties off while she unbuttons my pants. She pulls herself up while I pull my hard cock out.

The moment her tight pussy engulfs my cock we moan against each other's mouths. I know it's fast, but I pound into her at a punishing pace. She holds my gaze as I continue to fuck her.

It isn't long before I feel her channel squeezing me. I spread her legs wider—because my girl is flexible—and that triggers her orgasm as I slip even further inside her.

Heidi moans and bucks against me. Her pussy squeezes me so tight, I feel it all the way to my balls. It isn't long before I plant myself deep inside of her, coming so hard I swear my knees are going to buckle.

I lean into her, kissing her softly as I move my softening cock in and out of her. Our tongues dance, and fuck, my girl can kiss. I still remember the first time we kissed.

We were on the swings at the park by her house. I'd taken her out for ice cream. Heidi was in the prettiest pink dress.

I watch Heidi out of the corner of my eye as she swings back and forth. Shit, she's pretty. Her blonde hair flies out behind her as she leans back.

Suddenly she slips off the back of the swing and lands with a loud "thud." I jump off my swing and run to her. The way her body shakes I think she's crying, but when I pull her hands away from her face I see that she's laughing.

I smile down at her and chuckle. Heidi shocks me as she pulls me down and places a soft kiss on my lips. I take control of the kiss even though I have no clue what I'm doing.

When the kiss ends, I pull back and look down at her. Her cheeks turn an adorable shade of pink. I jump up and then reach down, helping her up. Since I'm not ready to let go of her, I wrap my arms around her in the moonlight.

fourteen

HEIDI

Colton leads me into Joaquin and Mona's. Today is the baby shower for my niece, Ember. I got her a bunch of little skirts and onesies with ruffles on the butt. Colton got her a little pink football that is adorable.

Iris and Max race down the hall toward us. "Auntie Heidi," they holler in unison. They hit me so hard that if Colton wasn't standing behind me to keep me upright, I would've hit the ground hard.

After I kiss Iris and she gives Colton a hug, she takes the gifts and skips toward the back of the house.

I smile down at my nephew. "What's up, Maximus." He gives me a half hug—he's too cool to be loved on, of course; unless it's Mona.

"Nothing, but I feel like I'm being strangled by pink." Colton and I both crack up.

"Hey, Colton. You're a really great quarterback. I want to play football when I get older," Max says as the three of us make our way further into the house.

Colton stops, and Max looks up at him. "If you want, maybe I can show you some moves."

He pumps his fist and then takes off running, calling for his dad. We step into the kitchen, and it looks like pink exploded everywhere. There are pink peonies, tulips, and roses, pink balloons, and my sister Mona is carrying a tray of pink cupcakes. If my sister made them, I know they're delicious.

The party is a blast. My parents are here, and I wish they would be nicer to Colton, but he told me he understands, and he'd do the same thing with our daughter; of course, that comment made my stomach dip.

Sierra is across from me with Ember in her arms. She looks so good for someone who just had a baby. Her thin figure is back with a slight post-baby bump, and her boobs are massive—lucky bitch.

My niece is gorgeous with her little tufts of hair, blue eyes—yes, they may change—but both Mom and Dad are blue-eyed so you never know. Ember has the cutest little lips and the sweetest little diapered tush.

Sierra looks up and catches me watching her. She gives me a smile and then leans down, kissing her baby girl's head. I blow her a kiss and get up to use the bathroom.

The door is shut, so someone must be in there. I'll just use Mona and Joaquin's. I step into their bedroom and see their bathroom door is shut, but I bet that's to keep Fluffy, their dog, out.

I grab the doorknob, and that's when I hear my sister, Mona. "Oh god, yes." And then the tell-tale sound of flesh slapping. Oh. My. God!

I, quickly shut the door behind me. I shake my head, giggling as I head back to the party. The moment I step into the room I spot Colton standing with my dad and Nick, and he has Ember in his arms.

He's a natural. It breaks my heart knowing what we lost. Shit, I have to tell him. I watch him bring Ember to his lips, kissing her forehead. My eyes burn, and I blink rapidly, trying to keep my tears at bay.

A hand grabs my arm and I'm suddenly being dragged into the living room. I'm let me go, and I turn to see it's Sierra. "Are you okay, sweetheart? I'm sorry. I should've thought this thr—"

I cover her mouth with my hand. "No, stop. I-I'm fine. It was a long time ago, and seeing Colton with her just did something to me. Now, this is your day, so stop worrying about me."

She cups my face in her hands and whispers softly, "I can't imagine my life without her. I'm so sorry you lost your baby, sweetheart."

"I am too." A tear runs down my cheek, and Sierra wipes it away with her thumb. I step into her, wrapping my arms around her tight. "I love you. Ember is lucky to have you as her mom."

I don't miss her sniffles. "Well, she's lucky she has you as one of her aunties. Now take a minute and then come back out." Sierra kisses my cheek and then walks away.

I quickly wipe my face and take a deep breath. I head back into the party and walk up to Colton and Ember. "Give me my niece." I smile up at him and take the sleeping beauty from his arms.

Mom watches me from across the room, and her smile is soft. She comes over and kisses my cheek. "How did I get so lucky to have four beautiful daughters, one handsome son, two gorgeous granddaughters, and one handsome grandson?"

"You look great, Mom. Arizona agrees with you." She looks like our big sister, not our mom. Her and dad both. "Colton, your mom and dad are having lunch with us tomorrow."

He wraps his arm around my shoulders. "I'm glad, Mrs. Collins. I hate that I hurt Heidi. I thought I was do—"

Mom holds her hand up. "Sweetheart, I know you did. I'm sure it wasn't an easy decision to make, but I'm happy you're together now." She pulls him into a hug. "Stop the Mrs. Collins crap, and call me Kathy."

She steals Ember from my arms and walks away. Colton kisses the top of my head.

I wipe off the tattoo I just finished and invite her over to the mirror to check out her ink. "Oh my god, I love it." She smiles at me and then begins clapping and hopping up and down.

"It was fun to work on." She had three colorful candy skulls, representing her and her two sisters, tattooed on her arm. When we met to discuss her design, she basically handed me a piece of paper of what she wanted on each skull.

When I called her in to show her the design I came up with, and she squealed so loud everyone stopped and looked at her. She apologized, and luckily every one of our customers knows how it is when they come to Sugar and Spice, Ink.

Once I get it covered, I lead her to the front desk, and Lainey checks her out. She gives me a hug and a nice tip before she leaves. I head to the office to upload her pictures onto the website and our social media accounts.

I stand and stretch, then head out front. I grab my phone and check to see if Colton has texted me. He was going to do some weight-training today with one of his teammates.

It has been a few weeks since the baby shower for Sierra and Nick's daughter. She's still on maternity leave and loving every minute of it. I'm sure they'll make more frequent trips home to spend time with their grandbabies. Plus, everyone expects Mona and Joaquin to add to their brood sooner rather than later.

Greta sits on the chair in Sierra's station. "What's up, girlie," she says before pushing off with her feet, spinning the chair round and round. When she stops, she pulls out her phone and holds it up. "Guess who got invited to Coachella?"

"Really? That's awesome. Who invited you?" I swear I'm only a little jealous of my sister.

"You know that makeup line that I've been using, the vegan one?" I nod. "They're flying me out. I guess I'm their number one ambassador."

"Of course, you are. Everyone loves you and can see you're a genuine person who believes in the products she endorses." She only recommends products she personally uses and stands behind. It also doesn't hurt that she's stunning, and when she does makeup tutorials, she makes it look effortless. Hell, she taught me how to wear my makeup, and I'm nowhere near as good as her.

"Will you help me put some outfits together?" She gets up and plops down on my chair, and I begin playing with her hair.

"For sure, but you don't need my help."

Greta tips her head back. "I know, but I miss you. You're always with Colton." She holds up her hands. "It's not like there is anything wrong with that—I love him—but I miss you."

I wrap my arms around her, resting my chin on her shoulder. "I miss you too, and tonight we'll find you some hot festival looks." I kiss her cheek and then I grab my next client.

fifteen

COLTON

I pull into the parking lot of Urban Fusion. I'm meeting Nick, Joaquin, and Miles for lunch. Heidi thought it might be a good chance to get to know Joaquin better, and make nice with her brother, since he still gives me the stink eye whenever I'm around.

Once I'm inside the restaurant, I spot the guys in the bar. "Gentlemen." I announce as I approach the table.

They all stand to greet me, exchanging a handshake with Joaquin and a reluctant Miles, and a bro hug from Nick.

"We didn't get to talk much at the shower, but congrats on the Tigers. That's incredible," Joaquin says as we take our seats.

"Yeah, I honestly thought I'd never get this chance after the cancer. I've already stepped up my workouts, and some of my teammates are going to work with me." I order a beer from the waitress.

Nick grabs my shoulder, giving it a shake. "Although my time with the Fire is going to be coming to an end, you know you can still use the facilities. We're all so damn happy for you."

I shake my head. "Okay enough about me." I turn to Miles. "I love your books. I don't get a lot of time to read, but I've read a couple. I knew you wrote in high school, but I didn't realize how talented you were." Fuck, I sound like I'm trying to kiss his ass. I'm a little intimidated by him, but that's only because I know how protective he is over his sisters.

"Thanks. I appreciate that. I love what I do."

The waiter comes, and Nick stands. "Guys, let me order for you."

We all agree, and he follows the waiter into the back.

Once Nick rejoins us, our waiter brings another round of drinks. We talk about everything and nothing. These guys are all close, which is what I want to be with them. If things keep going well with Heidi and me, then I hope to have a similar relationship with all three of them.

It takes three of the waitstaff to bring out our food when it's ready. My mouth waters as I look at the platters they set in the middle of our table. They place plates in front of each of us as Nick tells us what everything is.

"We have watermelon salad—I know that sounds weird, but trust me, it is delicious. We have sliced filets with grilled shrimp and mushrooms. Over here is salmon with a lime crema. The last platter is three cheese stuffed shells."

We all dig in, taking a little of each dish. c

Conversation is absent as we all stuff our faces. Everything tastes so delicious, and the meat is so tender I can cut it with my fork.

"What do you guys think?" Nick asks. "Amazing, right?"

Nodding in agreement, we continue stuffing our faces.

Once we're all done, the waiter clears our plates. Joaquin reaches inside his suit jacket and sets a velvet box on the table. "I'm proposing to Mona tonight."

We all congratulate him. Apparently the kids are staying with Miles tonight, so Joaquin and Mona can have privacy. If I had my way, I'd propose to Heidi tomorrow, but I feel like she hasn't given herself fully to me.

There's still something in her eyes, and I can't put my finger on it. We all stand to leave. Nick refuses to take money for the food, so we all leave a hefty tip for the waiter.

Joaquin is the first to leave, Nick disappears inside to talk to one of the managers, and that leaves Miles and me waiting for our vehicles. "Listen, I know you were trying to protect my sister. I can forgive you for breaking her heart, but if you ever do it again, I will take you out."

"Understood, and I hope I never do."

His SUV pulls up, with mine coming up right behind it. We shake hands, get in our vehicles, and then we both pull away.

Heidi's pink hair tickles my chest as we lie on my sofa watching New Girl. This is the only day we've really gotten to see each other in the past two weeks. Between my workouts and part-time job as a physical therapy assistant, we haven't seen each other.

Don't get me wrong, at night or early in the morning we'd make love, but not much more than that. It's only temporary, but it still sucks. I rub my hand up and down her back.

Her stomach growls, making me smile. "Hungry?"

"I could eat," Heidi says as she pushes herself up on my chest.

"Should we order a pizza?" I reach up, kissing her lips.

"That sounds really good."

I climb off the sofa and grab my phone, pulling up the app. After ordering the pizza, I climb on the sofa and pull Heidi until she's on top of me. "We have forty-five minutes to an hour."

She snuggles under my chin and turns on our show. This is how we lay until the doorbell rings. After I answer the door and take the pizza from the delivery driver, I place the pizza on the coffee table, and we sit snuggled together while we eat.

We finish eating, and she cleans up the mess. She comes over and kneels on the floor next to me. I rub my hand over her hair. "What's going on, baby?"

Heidi grabs my hands. "There's something I want to tell you."

I don't miss the way she trembles. Oh god, is she going to break things off with me? "O-okay. What is it?"

She lays her head on my shoulder. "It wasn't long after you left that I found out I was pregnant." I freeze. "I was prepared to do it alone because I didn't think you'd want the baby." She's silent for a moment. I can feel her palms begin to sweat. "I was home by myself. I hadn't told anyone I was pregnant yet because I wanted to go to the doctor and have everything confirmed. Well, I was taking a shower when my stomach started cramping. When I looked down, blood was running down my leg. I got dressed and drove myself to the ER. I'd had a miscarriage... I lost our baby."

I stand suddenly and accidentally knock her to her butt. "Fuck, I'm sorry." Bending down, I grab her hands and pull her up to her feet. I don't know what to say, but I feel like I'm going to throw up.

She lost our baby, and I wasn't there. I can't breathe. It feels like someone is sitting on my chest. I back away from her as a weird buzzing starts in my ears.

"Colton? Say something?" Heidi's voice is soft and broken.

I open and close my mouth, but no sound comes out. I turn on my heel, grab my keys, and bolt out the door. I look in the rearview mirror and find Heidi standing in the driveway.

I drive and drive and then find myself on Tyrell's street. It's not late, so hopefully it's okay that I stop by.

Before I even reach his front porch, the door is swinging open. "Hey, man, everything okay?" Shaking my head, he leads me inside. "Moni, Colton and I are heading to the man cave."

She steps out of the family room, takes one look at me, and wraps her arms around me before heading back into the family room, probably where their kids are.

As soon as we step inside Ty's man cave, I turn around. "She was pregnant. I left her, and she was pregnant with my baby." I scrub my hands over my face. "She was all alone when she lost it." I collapse in one of the armchairs. "How can she ever forgive me for that?"

Ty sits across from me. "Fuck, I'm so sorry, brother." He reaches out and grabs my shoulder. "She's obviously forgiven you, man."

"I don't think I can forgive myself," I say softly.

sixteen

HEIDI

The bed moves, and then I feel arms wrap around me. I begin to cry again, even though I thought for sure I was all cried out. Colton rolls me over so we are chest to chest. I bury my face in his bare chest.

"Shh…. I'm so sorry I left, baby. I was so upset with myself. I'll never forgive myself for leaving and making you go through losing our baby all by yourself." He begins to cry quietly. I wrap my arms around him, letting him get it out.

Together, in the dark of his room, we mourn what we lost. I'm not sure when I fall asleep, but it's with Colton wrapped around me.

The moment I open my eyes, I know I'm alone. I slide my hand across the bed and feel his side is cold. I climb out of bed and head into the bathroom. After using the toilet, I wash my hands, and then hold in a scream the minute I get a good look at myself.

My hair is a pink cloud on top of my head, my eyes are blood shot and puffy, and I have dried drool on my cheek. I splash cold water on my face a few times until the cobwebs are cleared away.

I leave the bathroom and go search out Colton. I find him sitting on his back deck, on the steps, staring out across the yard. I open the back door and walk across the wood.

I sit behind him, my legs on both sides of him, and wrap my arms around his stomach. "What are you doing out here?" I ask quietly.

He shrugs. "I couldn't sleep."

Resting my forehead against his back, I'm not sure what's going through his head right now, but I hate that he's beating himself up. "You know it wasn't your fault. It wasn't my fault either."

"I should've been there holding your hand while you went through it."

I get up and move around to face him, but he refuses to look at me. Grabbing his face, I tilt it up so he's looking at me. "Baby, listen to me." Colton does a slow blink and then nods once. "We can't go back. It's over, it happened, and we have to move on." I brush his hair back. "I love you. I've forgiven you, and you need to forgive yourself."

I pad across the deck toward the door, but turn back to Colton and say, "I'm going back to bed. I hope you come join me. I want to fall asleep in your arms."

I head back to his bedroom, shutting the door behind me. I sit on the side of the bed, hoping that he's right behind me. After five minutes I give up and crawl into bed feeling defeated.

I'm in that space between sleep and awake when I feel the bed shift. Colton wastes no time pulling me into his arms. "I just need a little time, baby. I love you."

I wrap my arm around his waist and snuggle up under his chin. In no time, my eyes get heavy.

Colton sits next to me, leaning down and kissing Ember on the head. We're babysitting not only the baby, but Iris and Max too, while Sierra, Mona, Miles and their partners are having dinner together.

We were invited too, but I offered to babysit so the new parents—Nick and Sierra—could have a night out with other adults. Of course, Colton wanted to come with me, and now we are at Mona and Joaquin's.

Iris and Max are lying on the floor, and we're watching Ant Man, because Paul Rudd is yummy, hello. Ember is snoozing, unbothered by the action on the TV screen; her little pacifier moves as she sucks it.

Colton leans down. "Have you heard from Greta?" She left the day before for California.

"She called me this morning. They were getting ready to eat and then head to the festival."

He wraps his arm around my shoulders and hugs me and Ember into his side. "I want to give you as many of *her* that you want?" Colton signals to the snoozing girl in my arms.

"I want that too." I tip my back to look at him.

Resting his forehead against mine, he sighs. "Is it crazy that I want to start trying now," he says before kissing me softly on the lips.

"Okay." I don't even need to think about it. I don't care that it's too soon—I love him.

His lips tip up into a smile that makes him look so beautiful it takes my breath away.

"Oh my god." We turn as Sierra, Mona, and Victoria run in, followed by the guys. Sierra holds out her phone. "Look who is right next to our sister."

Nick takes Ember from me, and I take the phone, enlarging the picture. "I-Is that Jett Hamilton?"

"It totally is. Do you believe it? Our sister is hanging out with a movie star."

I jump up, and we all start squealing quietly so we don't wake Ember. I'm not sure what he's doing standing by her, but I can't wait to hear that story.

"Are you going to come for me?" Colton whispers into my ear, making my belly flip. "Just think, when I cum inside you, I could be putting my baby inside you."

That triggers my orgasm. I arch beneath him and cry out as my pussy clenches around his cock. He thrusts inside me, once, twice, and then buries himself to the root.

I can feel it as he comes inside me. Grabbing his face, I pull him down and kiss him slowly. Colton grabs my ass cheeks, and with his cock still buried inside me, he rolls us so he is on his back with me straddling him.

"I want a little boy," I say, looking down at him, smiling. "I want to stand on the deck and watch you throw the football with him."

His soft cock slips from my pussy as he shakes his head. "Nope, a little girl who looks just like you. I'll be wrapped around her teeny, tiny finger."

I lay on top of him, my breasts pressed against his slick chest. "I never thought I'd have this again with you," I say and then kiss over his heart.

"Thank you for giving me another chance." Colton kisses my forehead. "I love you."

He moves me around until I'm draped across his chest. The beating of his heart soothes me to my soul. It doesn't take me long before I feel my eyes get heavy.

I'm officially moving in with Colton today. I know it's sudden, but we have a lot of history, a lot of love. We have five years to catch up on, and he's not messing around.

Greta and I have talked, and for now she's going to keep the apartment, even though... Well, I'm not going to share her story. I'll let her tell that one, and it's a doozy.

I drag my suitcase into *our* bedroom and lift it onto the bed. Colton walks in carrying my duffle bag and sets it on the bed. He pulls me into his arms and kisses my neck. "My baby is home."

He's been getting back to his normal self, which makes me happy. I hated seeing him blame himself for the miscarriage. It wasn't meant to be, and every day I hope and pray that when I get pregnant again, I'll carry the baby to term.

I turn in his arms. "I'm home." He kisses me deep, and then he helps me unpack. It takes no time to get all my clothes unpacked. While I hang up the last of my clothes, Colton orders us some Thai for dinner.

I put the suitcase and bag in the laundry room, like he told me, and find him in the kitchen drinking a bottle of water. He hands me one when I reach him. "Thank you, and thank you for helping me move my stuff in."

"Of course." He leans down and kisses me. "The Tigers emailed me."

I can't contain my excitement—I'm so thrilled for him. "Really? What did they say?"

"They're sending me a packet of information. I'll have to show up for training camp a week before the regular players. I'll need to have a physical, they'll run drills with me, and then I'll play with some of the guys. They could sign me or cut me at any time."

I throw my arms around him, smiling up at him. "You know you're going to make it, right?"

Colton leans down and kisses me softly. "Are you gonna move to Tennessee with me?"

"Of course. I'd go anywhere with you." It's the god's honest truth. I would've gone anywhere with him when we were eighteen. That's how much I love him. My sisters will support me and whatever I need to do for myself.

"Thank you, baby." Colton kisses me one more time before the doorbell rings, alerting us to the arrival of our food.

We eat in bed while watching The League, and then we celebrate late into the night.

seventeen

COLTON

"Okay, Mr. Johnson, let's head back to your room." My hand is wrapped around the gait belt at the older gentleman's waist. I've worked here at Roosevelt nursing and rehab as a physical therapy assistant for the past month; I'm just temporary.

Until I know for sure what is going to happen with the Tigers, there is no point committing to a full-time position. I enjoy what I do, and honestly, if I couldn't play football anymore, I'd go back to school to become a physical therapist.

I get my patient settled into his bed and quickly note his treatment in his chart. "I'll see you next week."

He gives me a wave and then turns on the TV. I head out to the nurses' station and look up my next patient's chart.

"Colton?" I turn toward the feminine voice; Lindsey

walks up. "How are you?" She's flirted with me since day one being here, but I ignore it. She knows I have a girlfriend who will eventually be my wife, but that doesn't stop her.

"I'm good. Just getting ready to see my last patient. How are you?" I stand and grab my gait belt, and she tells me, in great detail, about her weekend. I'm polite but start moving away from her.

Luckily one of the aides needs her, and she walks away. Down the hall I knock on my next patient's door and then get to work.

At the end of my shift, I grab my lunch bag out of the breakroom and head out to my SUV. I grab my phone and see a text from Heidi.

> **Heidi:** Hey, baby, I hope you had a good day. I made taco meat, and there's all the stuff for taco salads. I have consultations back-to-back tonight but will try to call you later. I love you.

I quickly type out a text to her, smiling because she does this all the time—making me something so I don't have to worry about dinner.

> **Colton:** Thanks, babe. I can't wait to eat. Have a good night, and call me when you're on your way home. I love you too.

At the house, I look in the refrigerator and find the food all prepped and ready to go in separate containers. She even cleaned the kitchen. It doesn't even look like she cooked.

I'm starving, so I heat up some meat. While it's warming up, I head into my bedroom and quickly change into basketball shorts and a t-shirt. In the kitchen, I make a huge taco salad and carry it out to the living room.

While I eat, I flip through the channels and finally decide on Sports Center. It feels good to know that I may still have a chance to pursue a career in the NFL. It's feels even better that my girl wants to come with me.

Things have been moving at lightening speed since we got back together, but I don't care. I would've married her the moment we reconnected. As teenagers we knew what we wanted, but I stupidly screwed that up.

I made a mistake, but I'll spend the rest of our lives making things right.

Once I'm done eating, I clean up my mess and lay on the sofa. It's been an exhausting week; between training and work it doesn't take long before my eyes get heavy.

I feel lips on my neck and sigh as a hand rubs my cock through my shorts. Opening my eyes, I watch pink hair slide down my chest. "You're home."

Heidi looks up at me and smiles as she continues kissing down my chest. I don't stop her when she grabs the waistband of my shorts; although, I do lift my hips a little to help her get them down.

She smiles up at me right before she licks my dick from base to tip, swirling her tongue around the tip. I watch as Heidi sucks my cock. Fuck, the first time she ever gave me a blow job I came in about thirty seconds.

I can't take anymore and pull her up my body to kiss her. While I fuck her mouth with my tongue, I reach down and unbutton her cut-off jean shorts. I slide my hands down the back and inside her underwear, grabbing her ass cheeks.

I have long fingers, so I reach down a little further, coming in contact with her wet pussy. I love how much it turns her on to blow me. She pushes down, causing the tips of two of my fingers to enter her.

She fucks herself on them, and her juices run down my fingers. Heidi is so warm and wet.

I need to be inside her. I wrap my arms around her and flip us so I'm on top. I quickly peel off her shorts and panties and then thrust myself inside her. We both cry out as I become buried deep inside her.

I grab onto the arm of the sofa under Heidi's head, using it for leverage. I thrust into her over and over. Her body shakes with each one, but she takes what I give her until we explode together.

Heidi pulls me down, hugging me to her chest as we both pant for breath. I pull her back so I can see her beautiful face. "Well, hello."

Her giggle makes me smile. "Hi. I promise I didn't mean to jump you, but little Colton was awake and taunting me."

I laugh as I hug her tightly to my chest. "Come on. Let's get cleaned up and then go to bed."

She climbs off of me, and I don't miss my cum running down her thigh. Why the fuck is that such a turn on? After we get cleaned up, we crawl into bed, and once I'm wrapped around my girl the way I want, I fall asleep.

I step inside my parents' place, and Mom comes out from the kitchen to greet me. "Hi, honey." I lean down, giving her a hug. "What brings you by?"

"Umm... well, I was hoping to get Grandma's ring." Mom immediately starts to cry, wrapping her arms around me. I hold onto her. I never thought I'd be here with her.

"Of course, you can have it. Let me go get it." She takes off running down the hallway, making me laugh.

Mom returns a minute later with a velvet box in her hand. "She would be so thrilled. She absolutely loved you two together."

I take the box from her and open it. A beautiful princess cut diamond, surrounded by tiny diamonds sit on a silver band. "Do you think she'll love it?" I look up at Mom.

"If it is coming from you, I think you could give her a Ring Pop and she'd accept it. Don't worry. Now, tell me how you're going to do it," she says as I follow her into the kitchen.

I take the water she hands me. "I'm not sure yet. I want to make it memorable."

"Well, do whatever feels right." She covers her mouth as tears run down her cheeks. "These are happy tears."

I don't stay much longer. I need to get this ring home and hidden in my safe before Heidi gets home from Mona and Joaquin's. They went to have brunch, just the girls.

I sit down and start thinking of my plan.

eighteen

HEIDI

I make it to the toilet right before I throw up. I grip the sides of the bowl as my stomach contents empty, over and over. Once I finish, I rinse my mouth out and brush my teeth.

I look at my reflection and smile—the positive pregnancy test sits on the counter. I'm scared, but so freaking happy. I'm not sure how I'm going to tell Colton, but I want to do it in a memorable way.

I smooth a hand over my still flat stomach and look up. "Please don't take my baby from me." I say that quiet prayer over and over.

Maybe I won't tell Colton until after I have everything confirmed by a doctor. I hadn't had my appointment with the doctor yet before I lost the baby. I take the pregnancy test and wrap it in a pair of my panties before shoving it in the back of my drawer.

In the kitchen I grab a Gatorade out of the fridge and take a drink, sipping at it slowly to make sure it doesn't come back up.

I get dressed for work, which is dark gray jeggings with rips in the knees. Up top is a pink, of course, t-shirt, with the Sugar and Spice, Ink logo in white on it, and a skull king and queen with our name in between them.

I give myself a bubble ponytail and stick my feet into a pair of black and white Vans hi-tops.

On my way to the studio, I buy some chicken noodle soup, crackers, and 7-Up. My sisters will think I have a stomach bug, which is perfect for now—at least until I tell Colton.

I pull into the parking lot and park next to Sierra's Mercedes. I swear between Joaquin and Nick, they're spoiling my sisters to death, but they both deserve it. Those two alpha males are all about protecting their families.

I grab my stuff and head inside. I spot Victoria, Joaquin's cousin/best friend and Miles' girlfriend, sitting behind the counter; she's been helping out since Greta is on her adventure with the movie star. "Hey, girl! Thanks for coming to help out."

"Of course. I was happy to do it." She smiles at me as I grab her hand, squeezing it as I walk by. The office is empty as I put my purse away. I put a peppermint in my mouth and grab my phone, sending Colton a text.

Heidi:	Hey, baby, I didn't get a chance to make you something for dinner.

I don't tell him it's because I was throwing up.

> I hope you had a good day. I'll
> see you when I get home.
> Xoxoxo

I stick my phone in my purse and head out front, sitting next to Victoria. I look toward the work stations and find Sierra, Mona, and our apprentice, Lainey, all working on pieces.

As always, I'm in a state of awe at what my sisters and I have built. We've worked so hard to put ourselves on the map as artists to be taken seriously. Our plan is that once Lainey is doing mid-size pieces, we'll bring on another apprentice.

The phone rings, and I answer it. "Sugar and Spice, Ink. This is Heidi; may I help you?"

"I was wondering if I could get on the cancellation list for Mona?" We go over what they're looking for, and I look at the criteria for Mona's list. I enter all her information into the computer and put her on the list.

After that, the rest of my night goes fast.

I let myself inside and find Colton sleeping on the sofa again. He does this every night I work late. I'm almost certain our baby was conceived on the sofa. *Our baby*. I rub a hand over my lower abdomen. I want to tell him so bad, but I don't want to jinx it.

I head into our bedroom, quickly changing into my pink spaghetti strap nightgown. In the bathroom, I quickly wash my face and brush my teeth. I rub moisturizer into my face as I head into the living room.

Very carefully I climb onto the sofa, lying on top of him. His arms immediately wrap around me, and he rolls so I'm against the back of the sofa, wrapped around him.

I smile in the dark when I feel him press his lips to my forehead. "Hi, baby." He slurs and then rubs his cheek against the top of my head.

Colton is silent as he climbs off the sofa and picks me up, carrying me into our room. We get settled in bed, him wrapped around me—my back snug against his chest.

His hand rests on my stomach, and I smile in the dark. I can't wait to tell him about the baby.

It doesn't take long before I fall asleep, dreaming of little boys and girls.

There's a knock on the door. I get up from where I'm snuggled up with Colton to answer the door. A FedEx driver greets me and hands me a huge envelope. I shut the door and look at the label. "It's from the Tigers." I am giddy and dance toward the sofa.

He sits up, laughing at me. "Give it to me, dork." I squeal as he pulls me down onto his lap. "Open it," Colton tells me, and I waste no time ripping the cardboard open.

I pull out the folder and open it. Together we go through all the papers. It tells him where to get his physical. When to report for training camp, his flight, and hotel information.

I turn to look at him and hold up the folder. "Baby, it is finally happening. My man is going to be an NFL quarterback." I throw my arms up and scream.

Colton wraps his arms around me, kissing the side of my head. "We don't know if I'm on the team, but I appreciate your enthusiasm."

"Baby, they'd be dumb not to want you. You're fucking talented," I tell him as I climb off his lap. After grabbing him a pen, I take pictures with my phone while he fills out paperwork.

Colton shakes his head as I keep asking him to look up and smile. "Hey, I'm just making memories. We'll want these for when you're famous, and you can remember when it happened."

"You're right, baby." He humors me and smiles, posing for picture after picture. God, I want to tell him about the baby, but I can't—not until I hear it from the doctor.

Once that's all done, we decide to order Imperial Palace because I'm craving crab rangoon dipped in sweet and sour sauce. I order our dinner as Colton sets the packet down on the breakfast bar.

"I'll call in the morning to arrange my physical and then I'll talk to whoever I need to, about working out my travel information."

While we wait for our food, we snuggle on the sofa and watch old episodes of Law and Order: SVU.

Little did we know that a month later our lives would change.

nineteen

COLTON

I sit next to Tyrell, watching Heidi run around his backyard while his kids chase her. Her pink hair flies out behind her as she laughs. It is no surprise the kids were all taken by her. She made sure to show each of them equal attention.

"She's great, man." He leans into me and says, "I'm happy for you." We clink our bottles together and then take a drink.

I make sure Heidi isn't close. "I'm proposing to her. I just don't know when."

"Wow, man. So many big things happening for you. I couldn't be happier." Tyrell stands and pulls me into his arms for a backslapping hug.

I return the hug, and then we back away from each other before Heidi sees and starts asking questions. Moni comes out carrying a tray of cupcakes. My girl walks up with the kids.

"Oh my gosh, Moni, these look incredible." Heidi hands one to each one of the kids before taking one for herself.

I fight my dick getting hard as she licks frosting off her finger. What makes it even hotter than it already is, is the fact that she isn't even trying to be sexy.

Heidi catches me staring and blows me a kiss. The girls sit at the table with the kids and dig into their cupcakes. I finish the last of my beer and head to the table to grab my own cupcake, sitting next to my girl.

We leave shortly after we finish. I have to get up early to hit the gym before I go to work. Tonight was the first night in weeks we've gotten to hang out. Don't get me wrong, I love Ty and Moni, but I would've liked the whole night to ourselves.

I hit the garage door button as I pull into the driveway.

Heidi meets me at the front of my SUV and wraps her arms around my waist. "I really like your friends." She smiles up at me. "I'd definitely like to see more of them."

"That makes me so happy, baby. They're good people. Those kids sure took a liking to you." It makes me a little sad that we could've had an almost five-year-old, but I look forward to any children that we may be blessed with.

Inside, Heidi disappears down the hall, probably to change out of her cute pink sundress. I fear if we have a daughter she's going to be drowned in a sea of pink, but I'll welcome it.

I get a glass of water and chug it down before heading back to our bedroom to change into basketball shorts and throw on my tennis shoes.

Heidi comes out of the bathroom in a dusty rose and gray nightie—it's sweet and sexy all in one.

"I'm going to go for a run. I'll be back in a bit." I lean down to kiss her, but she pulls back. "What?"

"You can't be serious? This is our one full day that we've gotten to be together in forever. I thought we were going to snuggle." She crosses her arms over her chest.

I lean down and kiss her forehead. "I know, baby, but I ate that cupcake, and I need to. I promise I'll be back in a half hour tops."

She brushes past me. "Whatever. Have fun."

I follow behind her. "Don't be mad." Heidi doesn't respond. "I'll be back." I sigh and then kiss the back of her head.

Outside I do some stretches, and then I'm off. I've never been someone who needs music when I run. I honestly love listening to the sounds of everything around me.

I'm starting to get a little nervous. I fly to Nashville to get my physical and whatever other testing I need to go through. I signed a release for them to get all of my medical records. I mean, they already know I had cancer, and they still want to see me.

Whatever happens I'm still honored that they saw something in me. I focus on my run, and after a half hour I head home.

I let myself inside and find my girl fast asleep on the sofa. I lock up and quickly shower. Once I'm in a pair of boxer briefs, I make my way to the living room and carefully pick her up off the sofa, carrying her into our bedroom.

I lay her down and she snorts, rolls over, and starts snoring softly. I smile and slide into bed, snuggling up against her back.

Heidi stands next to the back hatch of my SUV as I grab my suitcase and place it on the ground. I shut it and then pull her into my arms. "I'm going to miss you," I say against the top of her head.

"I'm going to miss you too." She wraps her arms around me tightly.

Things feel off between us, and I hate it. She's been distant—to an outsider they wouldn't probably notice, but I do. It hasn't been easy. We're both busy, or busier than we were when we started up again.

All I seem to do anymore is weight-training, work, running, sleep, and repeat. I will say, I'm in the best shape of my life. Heidi has learned how to make amazing, healthy dishes for us to eat.

"You need to move your car." The security guard pulls me from my thoughts.

"Yeah, okay; sorry." I look down at Heidi and smile. "I'll be home in three days."

Heidi tips her head back and puckers her lips. I kiss her hard, quick, and deep. I step back and grab the handle of my suitcase.

"I love you, and sorry I've been a crab. We just saw each other all the time at first, and now we hardly see each other." She looks so cute when she pouts.

I grab her chin. "I'll be home before you know it." The security guard gives us the stink eye. "Bye, baby."

"Bye." Fuck, I wish she was going with me, but they said I'd be busy.

I head into the airport, check-in, and then head to my gate. I could've, driven it's only about four hours away, but they offered to fly me in, and the flight is only a little over a hour.

I take a seat and wait for them to announce it's time to board. I pull my headphones on and listen to music while I wait.

I let myself into my hotel room. I'm exhausted. I had my physical today, and they drew lots of blood. I was poked, prodded, and monitored for hours. They're also reviewing my cancer treatment.

In the shower, I quickly scrub my body down and wash my hair. After rinsing off, I step out of the shower and wrap a towel around my waist. I go through the rest of my routine and head into the bedroom.

I grab my phone and quickly dial Heidi, wanting to hear her voice before I go to bed. Her phone immediately goes to voicemail. "This is Heidi; you know what to do."

"Hey, baby. I wanted to hear your voice. If you're still up, call me. If not, I'll talk to you tomorrow. I love you." I disconnect and then call my dad. "What's up, Dad?"

"Hey, son. How did today go?" My dad has been my ultimate hero since I can remember. He was my coach when I started pee wee football, until I started playing high school ball.

I let out a laugh. "I felt like a lab rat. It gave me flashbacks to going through everything back then."

"Ahem... I'm sure. Well, at least at the end of all this poking and prodding, you'll get good news. Your mom took Heidi dinner at the studio tonight."

I smile; of course they're looking out for her. "That was nice of her."

"I don't want you to worry, but your mom said she looked a little pale. I didn't want to say anything while you're in Nashville, but don't worry—we're all over it."

Fuck, is she sick? Is that why she's been cranky because she hasn't felt good? "Do you think I should come home? She didn't tell me she was sick."

"I'm sorry, son. I should've kept it to myself."

"Hell no, Dad. I would've been pissed if I would've found out. Should I come home?" I stand, ready to pack my bags.

"Son, calm down. You focus on getting through the rest of your tests. Your mom will go check on her in the morning."

My phone beeps, and I see it's Heidi. "Dad, Heidi's calling me now. I'll talk to you later." I switch over to her. "Hey, baby."

"Hi, sorry my phone died on my way home from the studio. Your mom brought me dinner." She yawns into the phone. "Sorry, I'm exhausted. How did it go today?"

"It was good. Now, tell me why Mom says you looked pale."

"I'm fine. I was just super hungry when she showed up. I-I didn't get a chance to eat lunch, and for breakfast I only had a banana. Your mom brought me a huge container of her homemade chicken fried rice. I'm much better now."

Thank god for my mom. "That's good, baby. I was freaking out."

Her soft giggle makes me smile. "Don't worry about me, okay? Now, let me go so I can sleep. I love you. I can't wait until you're home."

"I love you, and I can't wait until I'm home too." We hang up, and I feel a hundred times better.

I turn out the light and settle into my pillows. It doesn't take long before I'm out.

twenty

HEIDI

Colton texted me earlier to tell me that I didn't need to pick him up from the airport because his dad was going to do it. Now, I wait for him to get home, trying to ignore the hurt I feel that he didn't want me to pick him up.

I decide I'll make a nice dinner. The salmon and wild rice are in the oven, staying warm.

Tomorrow is my appointment with the OB, and hopefully they'll confirm the pregnancy, and then I can tell Colton. I rub a hand over my stomach and smile. I'm trying to be positive, even though I'm scared to death.

I sit on the sofa and lean against the back and cover my mouth as I yawn. In the books I've read, the exhaustion should ease up as I head into the second trimester.

I'm not sure I felt this tired the first time I was pregnant.

Beep, beep, beep. What is that? Am I dreaming? My

eyes fly open. There is smoke coming from the kitchen, and the smoke detector is going off. I jump and turn the oven off.

I grab the potholders and pull the burning food out of the oven. Dammit, I fell asleep and damn near burned the house down. I open the patio door and the kitchen windows to air it out.

It takes almost an hour to get the smell of burnt salmon out of the house. The smell has sent me running to the bathroom to vomit twice. I wrap a shirt around my head to cover my mouth.

I close everything up and go through the house one more time with the air freshener. It is when I pull the shirt off that I realize that Colton isn't home, and his flight was supposed to have landed an hour and a half ago. He should be here by now.

I grab my phone and call him. The call goes to voicemail. I call Colton's mom, and hers goes to voicemail as well. My stomach pitches, and I stand up. I put my shoes on and head out to my car.

His parents live close to us, so in no time I'm pulling into their driveway. I climb out of my car and run to the front door, banging on the wood, and repeatedly ringing the doorbell until finally the porch light comes on.

Cari opens the door, her eyes red and swollen. "Come in, sweetheart."

I follow her inside and into their family room. Colton is sitting on the sofa with his dad. He looks up at me, and the pain in his eyes causes me to freeze. I move toward him, but he holds up his hand.

"What's happening?" I ask, the worry evident in my voice. No one says anything; they just sit there in silence. Thanks to my hormones, I begin to cry. "Please, will someone tell me what is happening?"

Colton gets up and approaches me. "There's a chance that my cancer is back."

I reach out to hug him, but he backs away from me. "Okay... what happened?"

"My lab tests came back abnormal. My white blood cell count is really high, and my red blood cell count is low. The other day I noticed this." He lifts his shirt, and I see a purplish bruise. "This is what happened before."

"You're not alone in this." I reach up to grab his face, but again he moves away from me. "Stop it; we're in this together. I told you that I will always fight alongside you."

"Go home, Heidi. I'll be home in the morning."

"Why are you doing this? You promised we'd fight together. Are you telling me you're breaking that promise already?" I'm proud for the strength in my voice, but this feels like déjà vu.

I feel like at any moment he's going to tell me he doesn't love me anymore and break my heart all over again. I'm not sticking around for that.

"Please come home," I say before turning around and heading for the door. I rush out of the house and to my car. As soon as I climb in, I see Colton walking around the front end and climbing in the passenger seat.

Neither of us speaks as I drive us home. I don't know what to say, or what to do, and he won't let me touch him at all. Maybe if I tell him about the baby, he'll know he has something to fight for.

We get home and we climb out of the car, walking into the house. Colton locks up while I head into the bedroom. I get ready for bed because I'm not really sure what else to do right now.

While I'm brushing my teeth, he comes into the bathroom. He watches me in the mirror as I finish, and then he walks toward me. My heart races as he stops right behind me. His arm slides around my waist, and he cups my breast.

They're super sensitive right now, and I moan the moment his thumb rubs my nipple. His hand slides down my body to the hem of my nightgown. With both hands he lifts the pink silk fabric up to my hips. He grabs my panties, ripping them from my body.

Colton spins me around and lifts me onto the counter. He spreads my legs and steps between them. I reach between us and quickly undo the button of his shorts and pull his cock out.

He grabs it and quickly lines it up with the entrance of my pussy. He thrusts inside me so deep I cry out. Colton grips my thighs, spreading my legs even wider. My moan echoes off the walls, and my head hits the mirror.

I watch as he pulls almost all the way out and then thrusts roughly inside. There's a bite of pain each time, but I don't care. He holds my gaze as he reaches between us, rubbing my clit.

It takes no time at all before I'm coming. I grab onto him as he picks up the pace, thrusting harder and harder until he plants himself to the root. I feel it as he comes inside me.

He buries his face in my neck, groaning against my skin. I hug him tight, taking a moment to show him my love. Colton hugs me to him so tight I can hardly breathe, but I don't dare move. He needs me, and I told him I'd always be there, and I will be.

I'm not sure how long we stay wrapped around each other, but when we finally move he pulls out of me and quickly tucks himself back in his shorts. Colton picks me up and carries me into the bedroom laying me on my spot. He strips down to his boxer briefs and climbs into bed, wrapping his arm around my waist.

It's a long time before either of us finds sleep, but we don't say anything, just lay in the quiet.

I lied to Colton about where I was going—I have my first OB appointment today, and I'm scared as hell. All I want is good news, good news that I can give Colton.

The moment I step into the office butterflies take flight in my belly. After checking in, I take a seat and my knee immediately begins to bounce. The nurse calls my name, and I stand up.

After getting weighed and having my vitals checked, I go pee in a cup and then head to the exam room. She has me take my bottoms off because I have weird periods, so I'm unsure about when my last one was.

Dr. Honn opens the door. "Hi, Heidi." She holds her hand out, and I take it, giving it a shake.

"My sister, Sierra Collins, speaks very highly of you."

"Oh, I love your sister. How is that sweet baby girl doing?" She sits on the stool next to me.

"Ember is amazing. She is beautiful like her momma."

She turns to the computer and taps on the keyboard. "That's great. Well, as for you, you're definitely pregnant. You told the nurse you've had spotting every month?" I nod. "Okay, we're going to do an ultrasound so we can get an accurate age on the baby."

The doctor has me put my feet in the stirrups, and the nurse pulls a machine over. "Okay, Heidi. I want you to lay back for me." I do what she says. "You're going to feel a little bit of pressure."

She squirts jelly on the end of long white wand with a condom over it. I wince as she sticks it inside of me. I can feel her moving it around and I'm starting to get nervous.

Dr. Honn presses a button, and a fast-whooshing sound fills the room. I begin to cry because that is the most beautiful sound I've ever heard. "The heartbeat sounds great. Let me just take some measurements, and we'll see how far along you are."

She tells the nurse to turn the screen toward me. "Here's your baby." That is when I see a little black circle with a little white blob with something moving fast in the middle of it. "That's the heart." The nurse points to that spot.

"Well, Heidi, from the measurements, I'd say you're nine weeks and two days. That puts your due date at January eighth. I'll print off a picture for you." She hands me a folder filled with important pregnancy information, and she gives me my prescription for the prenatal vitamins. "This has basic do's and don'ts. When it's time—the classes you'll want to take, and how to pre-register at the hospital for when it's go time."

I practically float to my car. As I start the engine, I look in the rearview mirror before putting the car in reverse, and suddenly I feel sick as reality hits me like a bucket of cold water. Colton's cancer may have come back. I could lose him, and our baby could grow up not knowing his or her daddy.

I open the door and stick my head out, puking on the cement. I grab a napkin out of the glovebox and quickly wipe my mouth off. I continue the drive home and my stomach sinks when I pull in the driveway, open the garage door, and find Colton's SUV gone.

He was quiet this morning, which I can understand, but I'm scared he's gearing up to push me away again. The doctor in Nashville got Colton an appointment with a top-rated oncologist in Atlanta. He's young but aggressive. Colton will see the oncologist on Monday. I need to adjust my schedule because I'm going with him whether he wants me to or not.

I let myself inside and sit on the sofa. As soon as Colton gets home, I'm going to finally tell him that we're having a baby. I can only hope it fills him with even more of a reason to fight.

twenty one

COLTON

I stare out at Lake Clara Meer and feel so fucking lost. This wasn't supposed to happen—I beat it; I won. I'm trying to stay positive; it won't be confirmed until I have a bone marrow biopsy, and they'll draw more fucking blood.

After Heidi left this morning, I couldn't stand the silence. It gave me too much time think about the what-ifs. On autopilot I went out to my SUV and then ended up here.

I promised Heidi that we'd fight whatever came our way together, but how can I ask her to go through this with me? I'm gonna get sick, lose my hair, and possibly die.

A tear slides down my cheek. I take a deep breath

and head home. I see that Heidi is home, her jeep is in the driveway as I pull into the garage. Before I open the car door, I close my eyes and try to get my shit together.

I get out and move toward the door. The house is silent when I step inside, and I walk slowly through the mudroom. Heidi is sitting on the sofa, holding something in her hand. "Hey. What's going on?" I ask as I step further into the room.

She stands and holds her hand out to me. "Come sit." I take her hand, and she pushes me down to sit in the spot she vacated. Heidi sits on the coffee table in front of me. She sets whatever was in her hand down and grasps onto my hands.

Fuck, her hands are so soft. She smiles at me and leans down, kissing my hands. She lets go and grabs the piece of paper. "Baby, I-I'm pregnant." She holds out the picture to me.

I take it in my hands and can't hide that they tremble. It looks like a little white bunny. This is something I wanted so much, but now... How could we bring a child into this world, knowing that I could possibly leave them.

"Colton, please say something. You wanted this— we wanted this." She grabs my face. "Please tell me what you're thinking?"

I drop to my knees in front of her and lay my head on her lap. The tears begin to fall, and she wraps her arms around my head, hugging me. This is what I want more than anything, but what if I die?

"Please tell me you're happy," Heidi says, her voice thick with tears.

I look up at her. "I am happy but fucking scared."

Heidi strokes my cheek, and I cover her hand with mine. "I'm scared too, but I know together we can handle anything."

Dad helps me out of the wheelchair and into their SUV. Heidi sits in the back and helps me get my seat belt on. I'm a little woozy still after the bone marrow biopsy. Luckily, they give me really good drugs, and I don't feel much.

I pull my girl into me, kissing the side of her head. Before we're out of the parking lot, I pass out.

Heidi gently shakes me, and my eyes open. I find her smiling at me. "We're home, baby." She stands back so Dad can help me down. Mom leads the way, and my girl brings up the rear.

Dad has his hand wrapped around my bicep as he helps me inside. "Dad I can take it from here." He nods and Heidi follows closely behind me as we make our way into the bedroom. I lay in bed and after she removes my shoes and socks, Heidi joins me. I have a hard time getting comfortable, but she has me take a pain pill and that helps me get comfortable enough.

My parents stay to make sure that we're okay, and then they leave. We haven't told them about the baby yet, and we still need to tell Heidi's family about both the cancer and the baby.

Heidi falls asleep next to me, and I slide my hand over her stomach, resting where our child is growing. I close my eyes and ask whatever higher power there is to keep Heidi and the baby safe.

I sit across from Dr. Wagle. He doesn't look much older than me. He looks at his computer, where he has my scans and labs pulled up. Heidi sits next to me, holding my hand.

"Okay, Colton, I have good news and bad news. The bad news is the cancer is back, but it looks like we've caught it very early. I'm going to work together with my team to come up with an aggressive treatment plan," he says as he turns toward us. "I know you'll have questions once the plan is put together, but do you have any right now?"

My mind immediately goes blank. Fuck me, that sucks. "Uhh… I don't really know."

Heidi lifts her hand and leans forward. "What is the survival rate for the recurrence of this type of cancer?" Her voice trembles. I look at her and that's when I see the piece of paper in her hand, and I don't miss the way it shakes.

Dr. Wagle gets up and comes around the desk, squatting in front of her. 'We caught it early, and that alone increases his odds off beating it. That is all I can give you right now. I want to be honest with you—we have a fight ahead of us, and we'll do everything we can to beat this." He pats her hand before standing and going back around to his desk.

He calls his receptionist, telling her to schedule my follow-up. We stand, and he leads us to the door. "We'll see you in about a week, and we'll start your treatment."

"Thank you so much, Dr. Wagle." Heidi hugs him

I shake his offered hand, and we head out front to get the appointment card for my next visit. Heidi laces her fingers with mine as we walk to the elevators. I pull her into a hug, kissing the top of her head.

We take the elevator down and walk hand-in-hand to the SUV. I open the door for her, and she climbs inside, after shutting the door I move around the front to my side.

"You're going to beat this. Just so you know," Heidi announces as I climb inside.

I nod, not really sure what to say right now. I'm overwhelmed and fucking disappointed. Heidi grabs my hand and pulls it to her mouth, kissing the back of it. She lets go while I back out of the space and then she grabs my hand and we head home.

I let us inside and head down the hall to the bedroom. I kick off my shoes and climb onto the bed. I lay on my back with my hands under my head. Closing my eyes, I take a deep cleansing breath and try to clear my mind.

I feel the bed move and open my eyes. Heidi lays on her side facing me. "Are you tired?" she asks.

"No, just laying here thinking."

Heidi lays her head on my shoulder and wraps her arm around my waist. "What are you thinking about?"

I'm not sure how to say it, but there is a tiny part of me that thinks she's better off without me, and that's what I tell her. "You should be focusing on growing our baby, not taking care of me."

She gets up on her knees and punches my chest. "What the fuck, Colton? How many times do I have to tell you that I'm in this with you? It's you and me; we pinky swore."

I get up on my knees in front of her and pull her into my arms. "You're right. I'm sorry baby. I love you so much." I cup her face. "I'm going to fight for you and our baby."

Heidi grabs onto me so tight. "Yes, you are."

I pull her down to the bed. I situate us with her back against my chest. I wrap my arm around her, holding her tight.

"Are we taking a nap?" she asks, and it makes me smile.

"Yep, just for a little bit." I yawn. I've been so exhausted, but that isn't from the cancer; it's from not sleeping well at night, worrying about the future. My eyes close, and in no time I'm out.

twenty two

HEIDI

"Oh my god, Heidi. Why didn't you tell us what was going on?" Mona asks.

Sierra sits next to her, looking at me with tears in her eyes. "Sweetheart, we could've been there supporting you guys," she adds.

I knew they were going to be upset, but Colton and I needed time to come to terms with his diagnosis and celebrating my pregnancy. I look down at the sleeping baby in my arms and shrug. "We were so overwhelmed with the cancer coming back and the baby. I'm just thankful that they caught it early. We go next week to get his treatment plan."

"Well, whatever you need, we're there." Mona comes and sits next to me. "Our baby sister is having a baby." She wraps her arms around me, and Sierra comes over and hugs me from the other side. All we're missing is Miles, who is on a book tour, and Greta who is having her own adventure.

"Promise me that you won't tell Greta." They both open their mouths, but I hold up my hand and stop them. "No, seriously. She's having an amazing adventure; let her enjoy it."

They both agree, but I'm sure it'll be hard for them to keep this secret. We're close, and we've all always told each other everything—well, not everything, but a lot.

I don't stay too much longer before I head home and call my parents. That conversation goes well... ish. Before I hang up with Mom, she's ready to call Cari. Both of our parents are excited about the baby, and he/she will be something positive to focus on.

Colton's plan is to work as long as he can, but once he starts chemo he'll have to wear a mask while he's at work, to protect himself. It worries me, but we want to keep things as normal-ish as we can.

We're going to be adjusting our hours temporarily as Colton begins treatment. Luckily my clients are all super understanding and have let me reschedule them. Mona has talked about inviting guest artists to come work at the shop.

My sisters will work their butts off so I can have the time off that I need. That's the best part of working with family—we do whatever is necessary to make it work.

I start getting dinner ready, stuffed shells and cheese, homemade garlic bread, and a Caesar salad.

As I cook the sausage, my stomach turns a bit, but I try to breathe through it.

While the stuffed shells bake, I straighten up the living room and throw a load of laundry in. I look at the time and see Colton should've been home by now. His voicemail comes on when I try to call him, and I leave him a message. "Hey, baby, where are you? Dinner should be done soon. I love you."

An hour later, and he's still not home and hasn't called me back. I want to call his parents, but then I don't want to worry them. The oven beeping pulls me from my thoughts. I pull dinner out of the oven and set it on the stove top.

I'm too nauseous to eat right now. I pace the length of the house over and over until I see headlights. I move toward the door as I hear two doors opening. I step out onto the front porch.

Tyrell is practically carrying Colton toward the house. My man sees me and throws his hand up. "Baby mama," he hollers.

I move toward them, but Tyrell stops me. "Sweetheart, he's heavy. I don't want him to accidentally take you down."

I hurry to the door, holding it open for them to pass through. I direct Tyrell toward the bedroom. He has no problem getting Colton into bed. My man starts snoring immediately.

Tyrell and I head out into the living room. "Thank you for bringing him home. What happened?"

"I knew he'd had his physical and called him to ask about it." He shakes his head. "I'm so fucking sorry, but he's strong—he's got this." Tyrell pulls me into a hug. "Congratulations on the baby. That's great news."

"Thank you. What do I do? I feel like he's starting to unravel." I blink rapidly to stop the tears from falling.

"I think he's scared, but he tells me you've been so strong." He steps in and places his hands on my shoulders. "Hang in there, and if you need me, I'm just a phone call away."

I walk him to the door. "Thank you so much, Tyrell."

He kisses my cheek and then walks to the car that just pulled up.

I lock the front door and then head to the bedroom. Colton is right where we left him, and I sigh. I take off his shoes and then his socks. With quick fingers, I undo his belt and then button his pants.

I shimmy them off him and toss them on the end of the bed. Lifting his feet up, I pull the blanket out from under him. I get him sort of settled and then grab the hem of his shirt and pull it up, or at least trying to, but Colton rolls over and takes me with him.

I slide away from him, pulling the blanket over him before climbing out of bed. In the kitchen, I put all the food away and wipe off the counter. Once that's done, I remember there is laundry in the washer, so I switch it to the dryer.

I'm not ready to go to bed yet, so I grab my laptop and pull up Greta's Insta. It looks like she's on a yacht—the water is so blue it looks fake. Her brown hair looks almost blonde and she's so tan, but damn, she looks happy.

After I close the laptop, I grab the remote and I flip through the channels, trying to find something to watch, but I can't concentrate on anything. Mona swears by meditating, but I can't seem to shut my brain off.

After a half hour of flipping through the channels and folding laundry, I decide to head to bed, except when I step into the bedroom, Colton is taking up the whole bed. There's no way I can move him; he's all muscle and freaking heavy.

I grab my pillow and head out to the living room. I lay down, grabbing the blanket on the back of the couch and pulling it over me. Thankfully I'm so exhausted it doesn't take long for me to fall asleep.

A hand brushes the hair out of my face, and I open my eyes. Colton sits next to me, and sunlight filters into the room. "I'm sorry," he says softly. "I don't know what my problem is."

I could be pissy, but what good is that going to do? I have no clue what he's going through. "You're worrying me. I can't even imagine what you're going through, but getting so drunk that someone has to practically carry you into the house doesn't help anything."

He lowers his head. "I know, baby. I'm sorry; it was stupid."

I reach up and cup his face. "Tell me what you're thinking."

Colton's eyes look glassy. He swallows thickly and says, "I just got you back. I can't leave you. I can't leave our baby."

I grab him and pull him down so he's half laying on me. Neither of us says anything; instead, Colton situates us so he's against the back of the couch and we're lying chest to chest. I don't think there is an inch of space between us.

He kisses the top of my head, and I pull back look up into his beautiful face. "You're not leaving us, baby." I reach up and stroke his cheek with my thumb. "We're going to have a baby. A little boy you can coach, just like your dad did."

Colton shakes his head. "Nope, a little girl who's just as obsessed with pink as her mama." He closes his eyes for a minute and then looks at me. "I'm gonna fight. I promise you I'm not going to give up."

"I know you won't."

twenty three

COLTON
one month later

I stare at the bag of clear liquid and watch it drip into the plastic tube. Fuck me. I close my eyes and rest my head back. Heidi grabs my hand, gripping it tight. Today's my first treatment. I was nervous, but knowing she's right beside me has helped calm me.

Dr. Wagle laid out all my options, and we've decided on chemotherapy. Luckily, we caught the cancer very early, so we're going to treat it aggressively, but the road to remission will last another two years.

Heidi's been great throughout this whole thing. She's so strong and has been from the beginning. I'm going to make it through this because I have my girl who is strong as hell.

She still has morning sickness, and I made a joke the other day that if I got sick from my treatment, then we'd have to wrestle for the toilet. Heidi started crying and punched me in the chest.

I was trying to lighten the mood, but that was clearly a mistake ,and I felt terrible afterward.

I open my eyes and turn my head to look at Heidi. She's holding my hand, and the other is holding her phone, and I can see she's reading. I do a quick perusal of her body—damn, her tits have gotten bigger. She is still petite, but her lower abdomen is starting to look bloated.

The desire to fight and beat this cancer is strong. I want to be beat this so I can be there for Heidi and our baby. A wave of sadness comes over me thinking about the child we lost, but I can't change the past; I can only look toward our future.

Heidi looks up from her phone, smiling at me. "You take my breath away," I whisper.

Her cheeks become flushed, and she brings my hand to her lips, kissing the back of it. "Charmer. Do you need anything?"

I shake my head. "Nope, I'm good."

It takes two hours before we're finally finished. We're both quiet as we head out to the SUV, and she only lets me go to climb into the driver's seat.

I climb into the passenger seat, and she drives us home. When we step inside, something smells amazing. That's when we notice the containers on the counter. I pick up the note and read it out loud.

"We wanted to do something special for you. Enjoy your meal, and know that we are all here for you. Love Mona, Joaquin, Iris, Max, Nick, Sierra, Ember, Miles, Victoria, and Greta (if she were here)."

I lift up one of the lids, and a delicious puff of steam hits my face. Heidi comes and stands next to me, peering inside. "Oh my god. This looks amazing."

Inside is a chicken and pasta dish. I open the other and find garlic bread. In the refrigerator I find a salad and then a bunch of small containers. "Holy shit. These are all single meals."

"Ahhh, that's so nice of them. Now we don't have to worry about lunch or dinner this week. I also see some cheesecake in here."

We dish up some food on our plates; I'm going to enjoy food while I still can. Together we dig into the feast brought to us. Heidi makes little moans as she eats, and my dick twitches in my jeans.

At least it still works, for now. Fuck, that's a depressing thought... nope, not going there.

Heidi cries out as I make her come with my tongue in her pussy. She grips my hair as she thrusts her hips against my mouth. I bring her down slowly, and she sighs happily.

I kiss her stomach on the way up to her mouth. When I reach those delicious lips, I kiss her slowly and deep, letting her taste herself on my lips. Reaching between us, I line my cock up with her wet pussy and slowly ease inside her.

There will never be a greater feeling than when I slide into her cunt. She gives a little cry against my mouth that I feel deep in my gut. Heidi grabs onto my biceps—mindful of the wrap around my arm that protects my picc line.

I begin to move in and out of her, our bodies in sync. Her hands move to my back and slide down and grip my ass. I pull back and hold her gaze. Heidi clenches around my dick and gives a breathy cry as she comes again.

Her orgasm triggers mine, and I pump once, twice, and then plant myself to the root as I come inside her. It takes me a second to get my bearings and pull out of her. "I'll be right back."

I walk naked in the bathroom to take a piss and then grab a washcloth, getting it wet. In the bedroom I make quick work of wiping Heidi off, tossing the washcloth into the hamper, and then I crawl into bed with her.

She curls into me, and I wrap my arms around her. "I love you, baby."

"I love you too." Heidi leans up and kisses me.

"I want to marry you," I say in the dark, but I don't miss her stiffening, and then sniffles. "I'll be back." I climb out of bed and walk naked into my closet it and open the safe to grab the velvet box.

Heidi sits up as I approach the bed. She's smiling as I stop at the foot of the bed.

Damn, she's beautiful and all mine. "I wanted to make this special but, Heidi Elizabeth Collins, say you'll marry me—be my wife, baby."

She nods enthusiastically. "Of course, I will."

I slide the ring onto her finger, and it fits her perfectly. I push her back onto the bed and crawl on top of her. We get busy celebrating, and it's a long time before either of us falls asleep.

two months later

I hug the toilet seat as I vomit what little I had in my stomach. Heidi places a cool washcloth against the back of my neck. "Baby, just remember we just have two more months of this, and then it's just maintenance."

She helps me stand because I always seem to be a little wobbly after getting sick. My gorgeous, amazing fiancée is trying to be so positive all the time, and I've turned into a moody prick.

The fact that I'm in remission should make me happy, but it could still come back or show up. I still have to do treatments for another two fucking years. I'm just tired of puking all the time—I'm tired of being tired. Heidi is growing our son or daughter, and she's constantly playing nursemaid for me.

I'm unable to work right now. After the first month of treatment, I just couldn't do it anymore. I was nauseated a lot at first, and then I started getting sick. Patients don't appreciate it when you have to vomit in their toilet.

Our families have been so amazing. They've done so much for us; it's been incredible.

I focus on Heidi. Pregnancy looks amazing on her. She's rocking a small baby bump that is so fucking sexy I can't stop touching it. The baby is getting big enough that she can feel it move. I can't yet, but I can't wait until I do.

Next week we go for an ultrasound. They said we could find out the sex of the baby if we want, but we've decided to be surprised. She thinks it's a boy, but we'll just have to see.

After brushing my teeth, I pull Heidi into my arms. "I should be taking care of you."

She shakes her head. "You'll get the chance at some point, I'm sure."

twenty four

HEIDI

Colton naps on the sofa, and I watch him from the chaise lounge I'm snuggled up on. I take comfort in watching his chest rise and fall. These past two months have been the hardest to get through.

Between Colton's treatments, watching him get sick, and worrying about whether I might lose the baby, I'm almost to my breaking point. Don't get me wrong, I'd take care of him every day for the rest of my life if that is what he needed from me.

My beautiful man has lost twenty pounds since he started chemo. The nausea is daily, but the vomiting is only the first couple of days after treatment. He's been doing edibles, and that's helped him maintain his weight in between treatments. My six-foot-four, and normally, two-hundred and twenty-five-pound man is almost under two hundred.

I don't dare tell him I wake up at night and feel for his pulse because I dreamt he was dead. If I feel like I'm going to break, I go into the shower; it drowns out my crying.

I've taken a lot of showers lately. I'm trying to be strong for him, I am, but I'm hanging on by a thread. I feel selfish for even thinking about all of this. Colton's the one having poison put into his body to fight something trying to kill him.

"You're staring." I blink and realize I spaced out while looking at him.

I smile and stand, moving to lay next to him. His big hand immediately goes to the baby bump and rubs over it. "Did you have a good nap?"

He nods and kisses my forehead. "I did. Those edibles knock me out, but they give me the munchies, so I'll deal with needing naps."

"Are you hungry? I could make us some grilled cheese, or I can heat up the soup your mom brought over."

"How about both?"

That's encouraging. "Sure, but only half; let's see if you can keep it down."

He nods but looks ticked suddenly. He gets up and leaves me laying on the sofa. "I'm gonna take a shower."

Colton disappears down the hall and slams our bedroom door. He's cranky a lot, but everything I've read online says it's normal. I know he feels bad when he's like that, but it's hard because sometimes I want to be crabby too, but I keep it together for him.

I head to our room and hear the shower kick on. After leaving our bedroom I go to the back deck and sit on the steps. I cry silent tears because this wasn't supposed to be how our happy ending goes.

It's a while later when I hear the back door open and feel Colton sit down behind me. He wraps his arms around me. "I'm such a dick," he whispers against my ear. "You have taken care of me, and this is how I repay you, by making you cry."

I ignore him and get up, walking around him, heading into the house. I grab a banana and eat it as I head into the bedroom. It's too early to go to bed, but I'm exhausted. I quickly get ready for bed and then crawl under the covers.

I fall asleep immediately.

My earbuds are in my ears as I work on my client's huge back piece. He's wearing earbuds as well. This is good, though; I don't feel like making conversation. Colton and I aren't speaking, or I should say that I'm not speaking to him.

I feel so lost because I love him more than anything. I do, but I'm tired, hormonal, and worried constantly. I'm overwhelmed to say the least. Part of me wants to tell Colton how I'm feeling, but he's already going through so much that I don't want to burden him.

I focus on the piece I'm working on, letting the vocal stylings of Taylor Swift fill my head. Luckily it doesn't take too much longer before I'm finished. After I wipe it down, I give him the mirror to look at it.

"This looks amazing, Heidi; thank you so much."

I take the mirror from him and smile. "I'm so glad you like it. It's the perfect piece for your back. Let's get it covered, and then I'll send you to the counter."

Ten minutes later I'm wiping down my station. I have a dull headache and need to take some Tylenol. In the office I find Mona sitting behind the desk. "Hey, you," I say as I sit on the loveseat.

"Hey, honey. We haven't had a chance to talk—how's Colton?" She gets up and comes around the desk, sitting on the coffee table. "Is everything okay? You seem sad."

I bite the inside of my cheek to keep from crying. I'm afraid that if I start again, I won't stop. "I'm tired." I stand and move toward my purse when my ears start ringing, and my hands begin to tingle. My attempt to take a deep breath is thwarted when my vision goes hazy.

"Heidi? Hey."

Why does it sound like she's so far away? I stumble back to the loveseat, closing my eyes the minute I'm on my back.

Mona's face appears above mine. "Sweetheart, what's going on? I'm calling Colton."

I don't even have the energy to tell her not to; instead, I close my eyes. It's a half hour before I hear the door open. "Baby?"

As soon as I lay eyes on my man I begin to cry. He rushes toward me and gets down on his knees next to the loveseat. Colton wraps me in his arms, and for the first time in months I let him comfort me.

"I-I'm so-sorry that I've been giving you the silent treatment. I've been tired, hormonal, and worried. I didn't want to burden you with it." Fuck, I didn't want to tell him, he doesn't need this.

Colton closes his eyes for a second. "No, baby. I'm sorry that I was too blind to see that you were struggling. You're always so strong for me, but you're cooking our baby. You need to stay healthy for us." He kisses me softly and then pulls back. "Things have been stressful, and I've been an asshole, but I swear to you that I'm going to take better care of the two of you."

"We're a team, Colton. We fight together, remember?" He nods. "I promise I'll talk to you if I feel I need to."

"Good, now let's get you home, and tonight I'm going to take care of you," Colton says as he stands. He lifts me to my feet and then grabs my purse for me. "We're leaving your car here."

Mona comes in as we're walking to the office door. "I cancelled your last appointment. She said to call her tomorrow to reschedule." She wraps her arms around me and squeezes me tight. "Take better care of yourself, sweetheart. My niece or nephew needs their momma to be healthy."

I nod, and then Colton wraps his arm around my shoulders, and I lean in to his side and wrap my arm around his waist. We head out to his SUV and he, as always, helps me inside. He grabs my hand and I hold his as I lean back and close my eyes.

We pull into the driveway and I press the garage door opener. As soon as it is open all the way, he pulls his vehicle inside and then shuts the garage door. He leads me inside with a hand on the small of my back, making me lay on the sofa. "Now stay here." Colton returns with some hot tea for me.

"Thank you, baby."

We spend the rest of the night snuggling on the sofa, watching movies, and talking quietly. For a while we can forget everything and just be Colton and Heidi.

twenty five

COLTON
five months later

I stare down at my son, Cole, and still can't believe he's mine. Heidi and I made this beautiful boy, and I'm so in love with him.

He was born a week ago today, and thankfully it was a smooth delivery; Momma and baby did amazing.

The past five months have been insane, but it has made Heidi and me stronger. Two months ago, I entered the maintenance portion of my treatment, and I'm finally on a med that doesn't make me vomit after every treatment.

That has allowed me to go back to work, which has been great—my employers have been so good to me.

Now, instead of just walking for exercise, which is all I've only been able to do, I'm back up to light weights. I'm glad I'm starting to gain some weight. I no longer look gaunt, but I'm still a long way away from looking like I did before.

After Heidi shared her fears with me five months ago, I knew I had to get my shit together and quit wallowing in self-pity. I got myself on the right path and started taking better care of her, and I felt much better physically and mentally.

Don't get me wrong, chemo has taken its toll on me, but now I'm more myself and feel semi-normal. Heidi and I were able to enjoy the rest of her pregnancy. Since we didn't know what we were having, we decorated Cole's room in a light gray and light green. My parents and hers bought all the furniture, and my parents put it together for us.

We didn't have a baby shower, only because we didn't want to expose me to germs with my weakened immune system. Now that I'm on the last phase of my treatment, I don't have to worry about it as much as before, so we'll probably do a shower so everyone can meet Cole.

I stare down at my son and still can't believe he's mine. He came so fast that the doctor told us that she was going to induce Heidi next time.

Cole squeaks in my arms, and I bend down and kiss his forehead. He has tufts of dark blond hair and chubby little cheeks. Heidi's milk never came in enough, so we've had to bottle feed, which is good because I can help with feedings.

Once he's finished, I put him on my shoulder and gently pat his back until I hear the cutest little baby burp. I carry him into the nursery to change his diaper and then I bring him into our room, where he has a little bassinet that he sleeps in.

I lay him down and wrap the little thingy around him that keeps him swaddled, and it helps him sleep longer, thankfully. The little mobile plays soft ocean sounds for him.

Heidi stirs as I climb into bed. "Is everything okay?" Her cotton candy pink hair is in a haphazard bun as she pushes up in bed.

I pull her to me, and she snuggles in close. "Yeah, baby, it's all good." She falls back to sleep, and thankfully I'm close behind her.

Dad follows me into my oncologist, Dr. Wagle's office. I stop at the desk and give the receptionist my name before taking the seat beside my dad. Mom is getting some baby time while Heidi naps.

"You look better, more relaxed," Dad says quietly as he leans toward me. "I can tell you've put on more muscle."

I nod. "Yeah I've been working out with Ty. My appetite still fluctuates, especially the week after treatment, but I can deal with it."

The nurse calls me back, and Dad comes with me. They take my vitals and weigh me; thankfully, I'm up another five pounds since my last visit. The nurse directs me to an exam room. She draws several vials of blood and then covers the spot with a blue wrap.

We talk about nothing important as we wait for the doctor to come in.

Dad holds out his phone to show me that Mom sent him a picture of Cole sleeping on the sofa next to her. "He looks like you did as a baby. He is such a good-looking baby."

I smile and nod. "He's so chill all the time. He cries when he's wet or hungry, that's it."

"That makes me happy, son." He slaps me on the shoulder. "You were a pain in the ass." He laughs as he sticks his phone in his pocket. "Just so you know, Heidi showed me how to make a photo album on my phone. I titled it 'Grampy's boy.'"

I can only shake my head. "Of course, you did. Just remember that Heidi's parents are coming at the end of the week, so you'll have to share the grandbaby love."

"Oh, John knows I'll share the love."

Dr. Wagle comes in, and I move to sit on the table. "Hello, Colton. I hear congratulations are in order." He reaches out and shakes my hand.

"Thanks, Doc." I pull out my phone and show him a picture of Cole. "This is Cole."

He smiles and then hands me my phone. "What a handsome boy. Now, how are you doing? I know how it is when you're trying to navigate the new baby thing, and you're exhausted."

I shrug. "I'm doing pretty good. I've increased my weight training a bit, and it feels good to be lifting again."

"Great, what about the nausea and vomiting?"

"It's better. The pills you gave me to take after treatment seem to be helping. My appetite has increased, that's for sure." Heidi and I have started eating a plant-based diet.

We make dinner together, and we've played with recipes until they were perfect for us, and that's what I tell him.

"That's great. Foods that haven't been overly process are so much better for you." He examines me and finally peels off his gloves. "Everything looks good. We'll call you with the results of your lab work, and the next time I see you, we'll order a scan."

I shake his hand, and then we wait for the nurse to check me out, before we head out.

We decide to stop for lunch at *Urban Fusion*, and Nick is in. He stops at our table. "Gentlemen." I stand to greet him, and we share a backslapping hug. "Lunch is on me today. Order whatever you want."

"No, we couldn't, but thank you for offering," I tell him.

He starts backing away. "You can, and you will."

Nick ends up bringing out a variety of things for us to try. I only eat a little of each thing because I don't want to push it with my stomach. We end up taking lunch home to Heidi and my mom.

After my folks leave, I grab my girl and boy and pull them onto my lap. Heidi snuggles against me, and Cole sleeps peacefully in her arms.

This right here is what heaven must be like. To think I almost missed out on all of this. Heidi is so much stronger than I ever gave her credit for. We snuggle for a bit, and then Heidi lays Cole in the bassinet in the living room; she likes to keep him close.

She comes back to me, and we get situated like we always are on the sofa—me with my back against the cushion and her back against my chest. That's how we lay until we both fall asleep.

I groan as Heidi wraps her lips around my cock. We still have several weeks before we can resume sexual activity, but how could I resist having her gorgeous lips wrapped around my length.

She holds my gaze as she swirls her tongue around the head and then swallows me down. I hit the back of her throat and groan as she uses more suction. I spear my fingers through her hair, griping the strands as she bobs up and down.

Heidi gives a sexy little mewl as she sucks my cock like she's starving for it. The desire to come hits me too fast. "Oh fuck," I groan before I shoot my cum down her throat, and my girl sucks every little bit down.

She pushes up and smiles as she wipes a little of me off the corner of her mouth; fuck, that's sexy. I pull her on top of me, and she snuggles close.

"Thank you, baby. I can't wait until I can return the favor."

I smile as she nods and then yawns. "I'm sleepy."

"Yeah, baby. Get some sleep, just in case little man decides to wake soon." Heidi rolls off me and gets settled beside me and snuggles in close. I fall asleep shortly after, and I do it smiling.

epilogue

HEIDI
one and a half years later

Today is the day—Colton's last treatment. I'm not sure who is more excited: me or him. He's come a long way, but I'm so proud of him. This past year he decided to go back to school to be a nurse. He wants to work oncology or infusion.

I think to him it's giving back to those who helped us. For now, he's just doing his associates, but he'll do his BSN online. Boy oh boy, does my man look sexy in a pair of scrubs.

Our son is amazing, and I still can't believe that we were so blessed to have our little wild child. He started walking by ten months, and he hasn't stopped moving since. He's our little one-man tornado, causing destruction wherever he goes. My boy loves to snuggle his mama, though, and I love every second of it.

The studio is doing well. We were approached about doing a reality show again, but we declined. They not only want access to our studio, but our homes as well.

None of us are down for that, but we'd reconsider if it was just focused on the studio, and they abided by our rules. Of course, then they declined and that was that. That's okay, though, because a better opportunity for us could be just beyond the horizon.

My sisters are all doing fabulously. There are babies coming, and I'm excited to be an auntie again. I also love that our kids will all be similar in age and will be just as close as I am to my sisters.

I focus on the task in front of me and grab my Adidas and slip them on. Once they're tied, I pick up Cole and carry him out to the living room. I set him down with some goldfish crackers, while I double check my backpack to make sure I have a clean outfit, diapers, and wipes.

I grab Cole's bottles and shove them in my backpack. "Okay, baby, are you ready to go see Daddy?"

He stands and toddles toward me. "Moo, mah, kah. Da, doh, dee."

My grin is wide because I love his baby talk. "Yep, that's right, baby." I scoop him into my arms and kiss his chubby cheek. We head out to the car, and I get him loaded up. We head to the hospital where Colton is having his infusion.

I took today off because I wanted to be there when he rings the bell. I pull up to the valet and throw my backpack on before lifting Cole out of his car seat. He wraps his pudgy fingers around my pink hair and gives me a slobbery, toothy grin.

We head inside and down the long hallway toward the infusion center. The girl behind the counter smiles when she sees us. "Oh my gosh, is this Cole? Your husband said you were coming."

Oh yeah, I almost forgot. We got married six months ago in a little service at the park that we used to go to when we were younger. It was small and sweet, just the way I wanted it. We haven't had a honeymoon yet; between Cole and chemo, we haven't had the chance.

"Yep, this is him." I grab his hand to make him wave to her, and then he buries his head in my neck. "Are you being a shy boy?" He does his little babble thing, making the other woman smile.

"Colton is in curtain three."

I smile at her before heading to the back. As I stop outside his room, I see the nurse is pulling his picc line. Colton winces for a second and then she announces she's all done. She stops by me. "Hey, Heidi and little cutie pie."

She leaves us, and Colton stands, coming toward us. "Hey, babe." He holds his hand out to Cole. "Come here, baby boy."

Our son lunges for his daddy, who catches him with ease. "Dah, do, bah kah," Cole tells him and then snuggles in close, making my heart melt the way it always does.

Colton leans down, kissing my lips. "Hey, baby. I'm glad you came. Kara should be back in a minute to officially tell me I can go."

It's only another couple of minutes before the curvy redhead comes back. "You're all set, Colton." She hands him a folder. "You have a follow up with Dr. Wagle in two weeks." I take the appointment card, sticking it in my wallet. "Okay, guys, let's do this."

He wraps his arm around my shoulders as we head to a huge silver bell. I take the folder from Colton, and with tears in my eyes I watch him take our son over to the bell. It symbolizes the end of one part of our journey.

My man looks at me and smiles. With his eyes shining bright, he grabs the string and whips it back and forth, ringing the bell. I cheer and clap along with some of the other staff. Poor Cole looks around like we're all crazy. The nurses all come and give us hugs goodbye and wish us luck.

It is when we're walking away the Cole starts waving to everyone, giving them his big, slobbery grin.

We walk hand in hand out to my new SUV, a black Toyota Rav4, and Colton buckles Cole in. He pulls me into his arms. "I will see you at home, baby." He kisses me hard and then pulls back, smiling.

God, the man looks good. He's not quite in the same shape he was before the diagnosis, but he's real close. Hell, since we stopped eating processed foods, I feel like I'm healthier than I've ever been.

We head back and find a huge "Congratulations" sign and tons of balloons in our front yard. I know it was our families, and it makes me so happy that they were obviously thinking about us today.

Colton is smiling huge when he climbs out of his SUV. "This is great." He takes his phone out, taking a picture.

We head inside, and I can't wait to start celebrating.

COLTON

I ease out of Heidi's spasming pussy and roll to my back, bringing her with me. Tonight, we celebrated the end of chemo with a sex-a-thon that she initiated. My parents have Cole tonight, so we can be as loud and as crazy as we want, and we were.

I'm pretty sure her goal was for us to fuck on every surface in this house. We gave it our best shot, but after this—round three—I'm in serious need of a nap to recharge.

Heidi draws patterns on my chest, and it causes goose bumps to pop up all over my skin.

A thought comes to me. "You know, I think you're the one who healed me."

She pushes up and looks down at me. "What are you talking about? I didn't do anything that you wouldn't have done for me." Heidi kisses me and then pushes up again. "I love you, and I'd do this all over again if you needed me to. I'll always fight with you or for you."

"Fuck, babe. That's the sweetest thing anyone has ever said to me. That is why you healed me—you gave me strength when I was wallowing in self-pity. You stood by my side with no questions asked. Even when I was an asshole, you never gave up on me. Thank you for that." I grab her face, kissing her one more time. "I love you, my pretty in pink girl."

"Oh, I like that," she whispers. "You know you healed me too. My heart was broken, and you put it back together. You're my forever, and I love you."

I roll us so she's on her back and I'm between her legs. My cock is no longer tired because he's standing at attention. "I'm about to show you just how much I love you."

Her giggles turn to moans, and it's a very long time before either of us sleeps.

Nine months later, our daughter Harper is born and just like her momma, she's addicted to the color pink. Shortly after that, Heidi had the tattoo—*love don't live here anymore*—over her heart covered by a pink rattle and a blue rattle because my girl is filled with a lot of love.

author's NOTE

I hope you enjoyed Colton and Heidi as much as I did writing them. To be honest, I had no clue what I was going to put them through, but boy when it came to me, my fingers were smoking from typing so fast.

I just wanted to share real quick why there are some time jumps toward the end of the story. When I decided *what* was going to happen—it caused a bit of a hiccup in Greta's book. Hers will be happening simultaneously to this story.

That is why she is missing from a great deal of this book. I was afraid if I included her too much, it would give away what she was dealing with.

What does that mean? You'll get little bonus glimpses into Heidi and Colton's world, since Heidi and Greta are best friends—the same way Mona and Sierra are.

Anywho... thank you again for reading, and I hope you loved it.

stay connected
WITH EVAN

Facebook Author Page ~
http://bit.ly/2nGpUfQ
Facebook Reader Group ~
http://bit.ly/2osdDbR
Goodreads Author Page ~
http://bit.ly/2oo7iYH
Twitter ~
http://bit.ly/2nGiBon
Instagram ~
http://bit.ly/2nusgxW
Amazon Author Page ~
http://amzn.to/2nulojT
Bookbub ~
www.bookbub.com/profile/evan-grace

Sign up for my newsletter and get the latest news ~
http://bit.ly/2ncb8dv

acknowledgments

First and foremost, thank you to my husband Jim. Whenever I'm on a deadline, you always step in, handling the cooking and cleaning while I work. I don't know how I'll ever be able to repay you, but I'm sure I'll think of something.

Kaylee, thank you for always answering my many questions and for just being an amazing person and author.

To my amazing ARC team, thank you from the bottom of my heart for your never ending support. I know sometimes I like to spring those new releases on you, but you still give me your all.

Evan's Entourage, my most excellent readers group. Thank you from the bottom of my heart for your support and enthusiasm, I love you all.

To Silla thank you for helping make my story the best it could be and for making it look pretty for my readers. I know I was so late this time and needed a lot more help, but you're always encouraging and pushing me to be better.

Ben my amazing cover designer, thank you for making me the most perfect and most beautiful cover ever. It was like you crawled in my head and knew exactly what I wanted. This may be my favorite one.

Also a quick thank you to anyone who has ever read any of my books, thank you for letting me live my dream.

about EVAN

A Midwesterner and a readaholic most of her life until one day an idea came into Evan's head and a writing career was born. She's a sucker for happily ever afters and loves creating fictional worlds that others can get lost in. She loves putting her characters through the ringer, but loves when they get to that satisfying, swoony ending.

When the voices in her head give it a rest, which isn't often, she can always be found with her e-reader in her hand. Some of her favorites include, Aurora Rose Reynolds, (the queen) Kristen Ashley, Kaylee Ryan, Natasha Madison, and Harper Sloan. Evan finds a lot of her inspiration in music, movies, TV shows and life.

She's a wife to Jim and a mom to Ethan and (the real) Evan, a weightlifter, a home healthcare scheduler, and a full-time author. How does she do it? She'll never tell.

more titles from EVAN GRACE

REALISM:
Sugar and Spice, Ink # 1

"A single parent, opposites attract romance that will captivate you from the very first page"
- New York Times bestselling author, Kaylee Ryan

Ordinary, typical, conformed, are words never used to describe me. I've never been one to play by the rules. It's my world, my life and I do things my way.

I see the way they stare at my body covered in tattoos and my lavender hair, I just don't give a damn. There is only one thing in this world that can get me fired up, that's screwing with my daughter. As a single mom, it's my job to protect her, fight for her. She is and will always be my top priority.

So, when I get a call that she's in trouble at school, with a boy- no less, my claws are out and ready to strike. And the boy's father, some high society stockbroker, isn't about to deter me. I don't care how sexy, smart and rugged he is.

Opposites may attract, and I've been down that road before, it's one I never plan to travel again. A man like that would never be interested in a woman like me. That I know for certain, after all I'm a realist.

Chapter One
Mona

My alarm clock blares, causing me to groan. Those last couple tequila shots last night were such a mistake. Tequila has never been my friend, and I don't know why I thought last night would be any different. I push myself up into a sitting position, but that is a mistake because it feels like my brain is rattling around in my skull. I grab my head as I crawl out of bed and gingerly make my way into the bathroom.

After quickly relieving myself, I grab a bottle of Ibuprofen out of the medicine cabinet. I shake a couple into my hand, pop them into my mouth, and stick my mouth under the faucet. After swallowing them down, I shuffle back to my bed, crawl under the covers, and pray for death.

While buried under my blankets I feel my orange tabby, Peanut, jump on the bed, spin in circles, and then snuggle into my side. As soon as his furry ass begins to purr, I feel my eyes get heavy and let sleep pull me under.

I finally feel semi-human and climb out of bed, heading back into the bathroom. I brush my lavender-colored locks up into a bun on top of my head and jump into the shower. Once I'm scrubbed clean I feel more like myself.

Back in the bedroom, I throw on a pair of black leggings, white camisole, and a blue off-the-shoulder t-shirt. I pad through the house and stick a piece of bread in the toaster and brew some coffee. When the toast is done, I slather it in Nutella and then pour myself a cup of coffee.

Keys jingle, and the front door flies open. My reason for living comes running into the kitchen. "Mommy!"

I catch my daughter and lift her into my arms. "How's my beautiful girl? Were you good for Uncle Miles?"

My brother leans against the open doorway. "She was perfect as always. We had a blast, didn't we, Goober?"

"Yep, Uncle Miles bought me lots and lots of candy."

Of course, he did. My brother has been such an incredible help with Iris, but the man can't ever tell my daughter no. I set her on the ground. "Why don't you go put your dirty clothes in the hamper, and go play with Peanut because I know he missed you."

She kisses me and my brother before running out of the kitchen, yelling for our cat. I grab my brother a cup of coffee, and we sit at the little dinette in front of the window. "How was your girls' night?"

"It was good. Sierra was in rare form and forced me to do two shots of tequila after mass quantities of beer, and then I had to Uber it home."

There are four daughters and one son in our crazy family. I'm the oldest, then Sierra, Miles is in between us four girls, and then there are Greta and Heidi. We're super close, especially Miles and me. Maybe because he stepped in to be there when Iris' dad split, which was basically the moment the pregnancy test came back positive.

"I'm sure she had to twist your arm too." He stands and pulls me up into a hug. "I'm gonna take off. I've got a book to plot." Miles is a crime fiction writer and, the amazing man he is, a New York Times Bestselling author.

"Have fun with that, and thanks again for keeping Iris." I smile up at him.

"You know I'd do anything for my girls." He calls out goodbye to my daughter, and she comes running out to her uncle.

Iris launches herself into his arms. "Bye, Uncle Miles."

"I'll pick you up tomorrow from Kiddie college."

He leaves, and I smile down at my champagne blonde-haired, blue-eyed angel. "Today is a Mommy/Daughter day. We're going to make a veggie pizza, some chocolate chip cookies, and have couch snuggles."

"Yay! Can you polish my nails?"

I nod. "Of course."

She hops up and down. Her joy is infectious, and we start our Mommy/Daughter day, which indeed ends with snuggles on the couch.

At the end of our day, I tuck her into bed, brushing her hair out of her face. Iris gives me that smile that's like a balm to my soul. "Sleep well, baby girl."

"I love you," she whispers before rolling to her side and closes her eyes. I don't move right away; I sit and watch as she falls asleep. The steady rise and fall of her chest signals she's out.

From the moment she was born I've watched her sleep more times than I can count. She's the best thing I've ever done, and Iris makes me proud every day.

Is everything always rainbows and unicorns? No, definitely not, but my girl can handle anything thrown our way.

"What do you mean they want to have a meeting about Iris?" I look down at the paper that my brother brought to me after he picked up Iris from Kiddie College. He dropped her off at the tattoo studio I own with my sisters, just like he does every day.

Sierra and I started Sugar and Spice, Ink four years ago. We're all artistic and fell in love with tattoos and piercings. When I decided that I wanted to be a tattoo artist, I met with the one who did a lot of the ink on my body and got him to agree to mentor me. As his apprentice, I cleaned up the shop and answered phones all while learning to tattoo.

Sierra followed in my footsteps almost a year later.

Over the past four years, we've worked our asses off to make a name for ourselves. Because our studio is exclusively female artists, a lot of people didn't take us seriously. We had to work hard to get word of mouth referrals and prove we were just as talented.

We started getting followers on social media and really used the power of the web to make a name for ourselves. Now, four years later, we've been featured in Ink'd magazine twice, we've been interviewed on Atlanta's morning news, and we were even approached for a reality show, but declined.

I focus back on Miles. "I'm not sure, but they want you there tomorrow morning."

Miles and I step out of my office and head into the main part of the studio. I'm always in awe of the place we've created. The walls are a deep purple, almost an eggplant color, with white swirls. Our tables and chairs are black and chrome.

We have a lot of our artwork on the walls in frames. Some of the tattoos on display are ours, and Greta is on display for her piercings. My favorite photo is of the four of us girls in black Sugar and Spice Ink, sleeveless t-shirts, jean shorts, and red Converse. Heidi did our hair and makeup pin-up girl style.

We find my daughter and Sierra sitting in the waiting area drawing together. Through the entrance to the back, I hear the buzz of a tattoo machine, which is so fucking relaxing.

"Hey, sweet girl, why do they want me to come into the school and talk to them?"

She doesn't look up from her drawing. "I kissed Max," Iris says it so matter-of-factly that I'm taken aback.

"Who's Max?"

"Max Pena. He's my best friend." She has a smile on her lips. Man, I'm in trouble with this girl.

I sit next to her. "Did he not want you to kiss him, is that why I have to go in?"

She shakes her head. "No, he wanted me to," Iris says.

I don't have much longer to think about that because my last appointment of the day has just shown up. Since I have Iris, my sisters and I agreed it best if I open the shop daily, then I can get out of there by five or six, and I love them for it.

After my appointment, I clean up my workstation and find my girl in my office watching Tangled on my iPad. "Are you ready to head home, baby girl?"

"Yep."

I help her gather her stuff, and then hand in hand we head out to the work area and say our goodbyes.

Once we get home I make us some veggie quesadillas. Iris and I are vegetarians, which I wasn't until I was up in the middle of the night with a newborn and watched a documentary about where our meat comes from. After that, I just couldn't do it. I didn't set out to make Iris one too, but she loves to do what her mom does.

We eat at our little table in the kitchen, and she tells me about her day at Kiddie College. Things have been much easier this summer with Iris able to go there during the day.

After dinner, we snuggle on the couch and watch Modern Family. I can tell she's getting tired when she starts slowly tracing the tattoo of her name on my forearm. Sierra did it for me when Iris was a year old. *Iris* is done in beautiful calligraphy surrounded by gorgeous flowers.

Before she falls asleep, I maneuver her to the bathroom so she can go and then brush her teeth. In her bedroom, she changes into her pink nightgown with sugar skulls all over it.

Iris climbs onto her bed and under her purple butterfly-covered comforter. "Are you all snuggled in?"

"Yes, Mommy." I know my girl's tired. She only calls me Mommy when she's sleepy—much to my chagrin. "Will you lay with me?"

I crawl into bed with her and lean against the headboard. She rests her little blonde head in my lap. "Do you want me to tell you a story?"

She yawns and nods. "Tell me about the day I was born."

Iris has always preferred my stories over the ones in storybooks. I stroke my hand over her soft wavy locks. This is her favorite story, even though it was the easiest labor and delivery ever. "Okay, baby girl. It was two days before your due date, and I was working at a little tattoo studio by Georgia State." My mind goes back to that day...

My back aches, but I ignore it while I continue working on this arm piece. I've worked on this piece for four hours this go around and four hours a month ago. That time was just the outline and details. Today I'm doing the coloring.

I don't know why I keep working. My due date is fast approaching, and it's been so hard to work with my big, protruding belly, but I wanted to keep going as long as possible and to make as much money before his or her arrival.

I never expected to become a mother at twenty-two, especially a single one—no one does—but I'm ready and prepared. I'm just wiping off my client's tattoo. I let her stand and take a look at it in the mirror, smiling as she squeals with delight.

She comes back over, and I wipe some ointment on it before putting plastic wrap over it. I stand to walk her to the counter when I feel a trickle down my leg. "Oh shit."

Buck, the owner, is sitting behind the desk and looks up at my exclamation. The girl I just finished working on turns toward me as well. "Did you just pee your pants?" She laughs.

"No! Of course not, my water just broke." I turn to Buck. "Can you take care of her? I'm calling Sierra."

"You've got it, doll. Good luck."

By the time my sister comes to bring me to the hospital, my contractions are four minutes apart. On the way, I called my mom, and she's meeting us there.

Two hours later, I'm now dressed in only a sports bra and squatting in the water while leaning against the side of the pool, moaning through my contractions. I wanted a natural childbirth, and my midwife had told me about water birth, so that's what I decided I wanted to do.

My mom and Sierra help me through labor as my contractions grow stronger and extremely close together. As my stomach tightens, I rest my head on the side of the pool, moaning softly as my sister fans me, and my mom places a cool washcloth on my neck.

It isn't long before I'm hit with the desire to push. The midwife checks me and says it's time to start pushing. They have me squat in the water, and I begin to push. After pushing for a half hour, they have me reach down to feel the top of my baby's head. I moan as I push with all of my might, and then I feel the baby slip from my body.

They help me grab the baby, and as soon as they lift her out of the water, my beautiful baby starts to cry. The nurse lifts one of the legs and announces, "It's a girl." I begin to cry and hug my daughter to my chest.

Before my mom even cuts the cord, my daughter is latched onto my breast, nursing happily. I'd go through the pain of losing her dad and the pain of her birth to do it all over again.

"What are you going to name her?" Sierra whispers before kissing my cheek.

I've had a couple names picked out for both boys and girls and kept them to myself. I didn't want anyone to influence my decision. I stare at my beautiful baby girl and whisper, "Iris Clementine Collins."

Clementine was my mom's favorite aunt's name, and Iris because I've always loved it for a little girl's name, and it's my favorite flower. Both Aunt and Grandma lean in whispering their "hellos" to my beautiful baby girl.

"Mommy?"

I look down at Iris. "Yes, baby?"

"I love you." It warms my heart every time she tells me that. I can't imagine my life without her in it.

"Love you too." In seconds she's out, hugging her stuffed unicorn to her chest.

I slip out of her bed, turn on her nightlight, and shut the door. Out in the living room, I light my candles, turn out the lights, and grab my meditation pillow. I set everything up in front of the coffee table and ask my *Alexa* to turn on my *Chill Zone* mix.

On my pillow, I get into full lotus position, close my eyes, and clear my mind. I'm not sure how long I've meditated until I open my eyes and see that a half hour has passed. Peanut is sitting in front of me wearing the same bored expression he always does.

"What?"

He tips his head to the side and gives me a "meow". I reach out and scratch behind his ear and then yawn. His fluffy butt follows me as I lock the front door, check on Iris, and he follows me into the bathroom, watching me as I take care of business in here.

I strip down to my tank top and panties, curling up under the sheets and blanket. Peanut jumps on the bed, and I feel him circle his spot behind my knees before he settles in and begins to purr. Not long after, sleep pulls me under.

CHAPTER TWO
Joaquin

I pull my Range Rover into the parking lot of Edgewood Community College where I've been summoned by Mr. G, the head of the kiddie college that my son Max attends. My son's a good kid, so I'm not sure why Mr. G wants to see me, and my son has said zilch.

I turn to my boy in the backseat. "You ready to go inside, *mijo*?"

My mini-me looks up from his tablet and smiles. "Yeah, Dad." He shuts it off and sets it on the seat. I hop out and meet him at the front. Max may be seven, but he's an old soul. I'm blessed to be his dad.

I'm a single father and have been since he was a toddler. His mother and I were never right for each other. She was the daughter of one of my father's associates. She was a gold-digging whore, and I wasn't going to let her lead me around by my dick.

She trapped me by getting pregnant on purpose, but she's definitely not mother material. Melina hired a nanny when Max was barely a week old. I, of course, fired the woman because I grew up with nannies, and that wasn't going to be the way my son grew up.

Max only sees her once or maybe twice a year, and it's usually awkward and confuses my boy. His mom's remarried now and someone else's problem—thank God. My cell phone rings as we walk through the halls toward the office of Mr. G. I look and see that it's my secretary, Lauren. "Hold up, Max. I have to take this." I swipe the screen. "Hey, Lauren."

"Sorry to bother you, Mr. Pena." I roll my eyes because I'm constantly telling her to call me Joaquin, but she refuses. "Your three o'clock appointment called and said that they could reschedule for four-thirty. Correct?"

"Yes, as long as they're my last appointment. I promised Max I'd grill burgers tonight, and I don't want to be at the office late." Max smiles up at me, and I ruffle his brown, shaggy hair. I'll need to make him an appointment for a haircut.

"You're all finished after that. I'll make the arrangements. Shall I have coffee waiting?" Lauren is by far the best secretary I've ever had.

"That would be great, thank you." I disconnect and shove my phone inside the pocket of my favorite dove gray Tom Ford two-piece suit. My shirt is a dark salmon pink color, as is the pocket square, and I'm not wearing a tie. On my feet are my favorite Ferragamo Benson burnished leather loafers.

We turn the corner, and I notice a woman with lavender hair braided and hanging over one shoulder. She looks up as we approach, and I'm hit by some unknown force right in the solar plexus. Her eyes are a sparkling cornflower blue. She's got lips made for kissing—*made for kissing?*

Her sun-kissed arms are covered in gorgeous, colorful tattoos. Her white t-shirt hangs off one dainty shoulder, black legging capris cover her legs, and hot pink Converses cover her feet.

"Iris!" Max runs past me to the beautiful little blonde who looks like her mom's twin, but without the lavender hair and ink.

"Max!" She jumps up, and they hug each other. They move to the opposite bench, talking quietly to each other.

"Um… hi. I'm Mona." The lavender-haired beauty holds out her hand. I take her hand, ignoring how soft and small it feels in my much larger one.

"Mr. Pena and Ms. Collins, I'm Mr. G." I turn away from Mona and look at the short man with a major paunch and thinning hairline.

I don't miss the way he looks at Mona, what with the tattoos and the lavender colored hair; she doesn't look like a lot of the parents who bring their kids here. I hold my hand out, squeezing his hand a little harder than necessary. "I'm Joaquin, Max's dad."

"Pleasure," he says and then holds his hand out to Mona. "Please follow me into my office."

We both sit in front of his desk while the kids are led to one of the classrooms to give us some privacy. Mr. G sits behind his desk like he's all high and mighty.

The man looks between the two of us. "Before we begin, will Mrs. Pena be joining us?"

Had the moron read Max's information he'd see that she's not. "His mother is on vacation with her husband. He lives with me full-time."

The idiot nods. "Yesterday, there was a situation with your kids. It was snack time, and the children weren't with the class, so one of the aides went looking for them. She found the two of them by the bathroom, and they were kissing on the mouth." He crosses his arms and looks between us.

Before I can respond, Mona chimes in, "And???"

"Ms. Collins, we don't tolerate that sort of behavior here." The fat prick scowls at her.

Mona leans forward. "I understand that, but did either of them appear to be in distress?"

"Well no, but they're seven years old, and they shouldn't even know about that stuff." Mr. G stares at Mona with a judgmental look on his face.

Out of the corner of my eye, I see Mona tense, gripping the armrests of her chair. She looks ready to snap, and I do the only thing I can think of and put my hand on her knee. I don't miss the way she freezes, and I certainly don't miss the way she trembles under my hand.

I remove it and ignore the fact that it made my dick twitch and my pulse race a little. I open my mouth to speak, but Mona chimes in again. "They shouldn't know about that stuff? I beg your pardon, but people kiss in cartoons. My daughter sees her grandparents kiss. I'm not going to make her feel ashamed that she did it." She stands. "I will talk to her about sneaking off with her friends, and she won't do that again."

"Ms. Collins, I can see you're upset, but the kids aren't in trouble. We just wanted to make you aware of what happened, and maybe you both could discuss with them what is and isn't proper behavior in school." He stands from behind his desk. "I want you to know that your daughter is a joy to have in our creative writing class. She's got a natural gift."

We follow him into the classroom that's off his office and find Iris and Max sitting together coloring. Mona sits across from them. "That's a great tree, Max."

My boy smiles up at her. "Your hair is pretty." He's a charmer, that's for sure.

Mona reaches across the table and grabs Max's arm. "Thank you. Iris, come give me a hug goodbye. Uncle Miles will pick you up and bring you to the studio, okay."

"Yes, Mom. I love you."

I walk around the table, ruffling Max's hair. "I'll be back after my meeting to get you. I love you, *mijo*."

As soon as I leave the classroom I spot Mona up ahead, but I don't rush to catch up with her; there's no point. Like I said, she's not my type. Plus, my focus needs to be on my son, not pussy.

I head downtown to my office. I have to prep before my meeting. My partners and I keep things flexible, which is great and I'm able to get off at a reasonable time so I can still be a father to my boy. My father is a workaholic, and growing up I watched as my mom grew to resent him.

They both began screwing around on each other, and that led to a nasty divorce. Now they live on opposite sides of the country. Dad is on marriage number four, and Mom is on marriage number two, but things are rocky.

When I divorced Max's mom I swore, I was never going to get married again. She reminded me exactly why I wanted to always stay single, but I'll never regret my boy. Once I reach the office, I park in the garage and head to the elevator, taking it up to my floor.

I share a floor with a marketing agency, but they're on one side, and I'm on the other. My partners and I have had our own brokerage firm for the past three years. Before that, I worked for my father's firm. When he decided to retire down in Florida, his partners became mine, and his clients followed me.

Our receptionist for the office greets me from his desk. "Good morning, Shane."

"Morning. I love that suit; it's my favorite," he says with his usual flourish. The man basically runs the office and is my personal shopper. He and Lauren are the backbone of the company. I'd be lost without either of them. He flirts with me a little, but it doesn't bother me; he's harmless.

I shake my head and head toward the back. Lauren stands as I approach. "How was the meeting?"

"My son and a little girl snuck off, and when they found them they were kissing on the lips. Iris is his best friend I guess. Anyway, the guy was a pompous ass. Iris' mom let him have it."

"My boys were rascals like that when they were his age. I'm sure it was harmless." Her boys are in their early twenties, and even though I'm thirty she treats me like one of her kids, but not in an obnoxious way. "I've got the conference room set up for your meeting. When they arrive, shall I bring you coffee?" She follows me into my office.

"That would be great." Lauren hands me my messages and then closes the door behind her, letting me get to work.

Free on Kindle Unlimited

CHAPTER ONE
Lani

"Are you sure your dad is okay with me tagging along? I don't want to get in the way of your visit." My best friend, Molly, sits down next to my carry-on bag as I stuff my toiletries inside it.

She grabs my hand before I can zip the bag shut. "Of course he doesn't care. He said it'd be good if I brought someone just because he may have to run to the bar. Plus, he says that he's pretty boring and I'd want someone to go dancing with."

Molly's dad paid for my plane ticket, and when I refused to accept it, she made sure to let me know that her dad got non-refundable tickets. Molly told her dad that I'd refuse them—that's why he did it.

Of course he was taking a gamble that something would keep one or both of us from going.

"Okay, I am pretty excited to swim in the ocean."

I've never really been anywhere, and I've certainly never been to the coast. Growing up, it was just my mom and me. I never knew my dad, and my mom sometimes had to work two or three jobs to keep food on the table and clothes on my back.

I met Molly our freshman year at the U of I in Iowa City. We're both elementary education students.

Now we're on spring break of our senior year. She and I are both so ready to be done and get teaching jobs. Part of the reason she wants me to go with her to Florida is that once we're both out in the real world, one or both of us could end up moving away.

My mom and I have had the discussion multiple times. We're super close, but she also knows that I'll need to go where the work is.

"Hello?" Molly waves her hand in front of my face. "Where'd you go?"

I shake my head. "Nowhere, just spaced out for a second. Are we taking an Uber to the airport?"

"Yeah, I figure that way we don't have to worry about parking." She reaches out, grabbing one of my sable locks. "Your hair grows so fast. I'm so jealous of your curls." She's one to talk. My gorgeous friend has sleek sheets of auburn hair, sparkling blue eyes, and a willowy body—with great breasts.

Me, on the other hand, I've got dark hair and eyes, light tan skin and I'm pretty muscular. I joined Crossfit after I gained my freshman thirty. Now I've got muscles and I'm fucking strong. Molly assures me all of the time that my body is still girly.

I grab my bag and Molly stands up. We're dressed almost exactly the same. We're both in black leggings, long sleeve t-shirts with zipped up hoodies over them. I'm wearing a beat-up old pair of Adidas and she's wearing Nikes.

She orders our Uber as I carry my bag and tote out into the living room and set them down next to Molly's stuff. Nervous anticipation fills me because I've never flown before, but I downloaded movies on my iPad to distract me and bought some books that I've downloaded on my Kindle.

When the driver is a couple of minutes away, we lock up and head downstairs.

It takes us about a half hour to get to the airport. After checking in and going through security, we make our way to our gate. We sit next to each other—I pull out my Kindle and she pulls out her phone.

Molly grabs her bottle of Xanax out of her purse and breaks one in half and hands it to me. "This is a low dose. It'll help take the edge off."

I take it, pop it in my mouth, and wash it down with my bottle of water. My knee bounces up and down while we wait to begin boarding. By the time we're getting on the plane, I feel loosey-goosey. I follow Molly to our seats, and I give her the window seat because I don't think I'm ready for that yet.

When we're ready to take off, I ask Molly to tell me more about her dad. I know that he and Molly's mom weren't married for very long, and he owns his own bar down in Key West. They had her young, and unfortunately he moved away due to his job and she didn't get to see him as often as she'd like.

Her dad's supposed to be the complete opposite of her mom. Molly says he's a free spirit and a bit wild, but a good and loving dad. I've seen pictures and he's definitely hot. He looks like Samantha's boyfriend from *Sex and the City*. I'm sure the women hang all over him.

When we finally land, the sun is starting to set. I look out Molly's window and am in awe of the view. The water looks dark blue, and I can't wait to see it in the sunshine. As soon as the seatbelt light goes off, Molly pulls out her phone. "I'm texting Dad that we're here."

I stand up and stretch my poor body—fuck me, there's no room on these planes. Molly grabs our bags out of the overhead compartment and hands me mine. I follow closely behind her as we make our way out of the plane on to the tarmac.

Molly screams, drops her bag, and takes off toward baggage claim. I follow much more sedately and smile as she flings herself at—who I'm assuming is her dad. He sets Molly down and I smile as I watch him hug her tightly.

I hear her say my name, and then they turn toward me. My stomach does a little flip as he smiles at me. Oh God, I can feel my nipples hardening. What if he can tell?

"Lani, come meet my Dad. Dad, this is my bestie, Lani. This crazy man is my dad, Damon." Oh great, even his name is hot.

I reach my hand out. "It's so nice to meet you. Thank you for letting me come with Molly."

He grips my hand in his. I try not to stare at his beautiful face, but I can't help it. His square jaw is covered in light stubble. His blue eyes are highlighted by beautifully long eyelashes, and he's got lines around his eyes that just add to his gorgeousness. He's got that dimple in his chin, and full lips I want to kiss. *What?*

"I'm glad you could come and keep my girl company and you're very welcome." We follow him outside to his black Jeep Wrangler.

The wind blows through my hair as we make our way toward her dad's place. We pull up in front of the cutest little house I've ever seen. It's exactly what you'd expect a house to look like in a beach town. "You girls each have your own room with a Jack and Jill bathroom in between. Your bedrooms are upstairs. Mine is on the main floor."

We step into the house and I'm immediately in love. The floors are a light wood. The walls are a light tan-ish yellow with white trim. The sofa and two chairs are the color of watermelon.

I don't get to look too much before he shows us to our bedrooms upstairs. Full-size mattresses fill both rooms, but Molly's has pictures on the walls and nightstand. A teddy bear also sits on top of her bed. "I'll whip up something for dinner while you get settled."

"Thanks, Dad." Molly hugs him before he disappears downstairs. "Go get your stuff put away and get comfy. We'll rest until dinner is done."

On the way into my room, all I can think is that her dad is hot and it's going to be a long week.

CHAPTER TWO
Damon

I head downstairs, ignoring the reaction I had to Lani. The moment I laid eyes on her, I felt like I'd been kicked in the gut. I've *never* in my forty-two years *ever* had that reaction to a woman like this before.

Wouldn't it just figure that she's forbidden times two: She's my daughter's best friend and I'm old enough to be her father. I grab the salad out of the refrigerator and the chicken breasts I've had marinating all day. It's a homemade marinade that Molly and I "invented" when she was visiting the summer after her freshman year in high school.

We named it Monroe's special sauce, I know... real original. It's got red wine vinegar, olive oil, soy sauce, garlic, oregano, and it's got a real nice tang to it. I take it out and turn on my gas grill. Once I place the chicken on the grill, I close the lid and run the bowl inside.

I head back outside and take a drink of my beer when arms wrap around my waist. I wrap my arm around Molly's shoulders and hug her into my side, kissing her forehead. This beautiful girl is the best thing I've ever done. I tried making it work with her mom, but she was jealous and never trusted me.

Every time I had to travel and do a shoot, she'd accuse me of cheating, which I never did. It got to be too much, so when Molly was three, we split. At first, I was able to see her a lot, but when the modeling jobs started drying up, I got offered a job and worked for a short time at one of the TV stations here, but I hated it.

I decided to buy an old run-down bar that was no longer open. It took me almost a year to get it to where I wanted it and now *Molly's* is a hot spot. We're right near the water, which makes it a tourist attraction. We're nothing special, no gimmicks, no dance floor, but we still pack them in.

"Oh, is that Monroe's special sauce?" She takes a big whiff and I swear I hear her stomach growl.

"Of course it is. I bought a couple bottles of Riesling for you. I know you said that you liked sweet wines. Tomorrow night I'm throwing you girls a welcoming party. It's nothing big just a few friends that want to see you, and meet Lani."

She gives me another squeeze. "That's great. I've missed you," Molly says quietly. She's always been a daddy's girl even when we were far apart.

"I've missed you too, baby." Out of the corner of my eye, I find Lani standing a few feet away from us looking unsure of herself. "Lani, I hope you like chicken."

She walks toward us. "I do, thanks. Your home is really beautiful, Mr. Monroe."

"Nope, don't call me mister, it makes me feel old." The lights above the grill show off the pink tinge of her cheeks. "Please just call me Damon." I look to my daughter. "Why don't you ladies get a drink and set the table by the pool. Dinner will be ready in about five minutes."

Molly grabs Lani's arm and drags her toward the house. My eyes immediately go to Lani's ass in the little shorts she's wearing. Fuck, her legs go on and on, and... of course she turns and catches me staring at her.

Free on Kindle Unlimited